EAT, PREY, BLOOD

A Novel

ELIZABETH RUSSELL

Copyright © 2018 by Elizabeth Russell

ISBN: 978-1-7323362-1-6

Edited by: Allie Coker
Cover art by: Hana Russell

Published by Warren Publishing
Charlotte, NC
www.warrenpublishing.net
Printed in the United States

In memory of my grandfather,
Fielding Dillard Russell Sr.,
who shared his life-long love
of language and literature with me.

CHAPTER ONE

1

I wasn't going to be able to talk her out of it. My mother was sending me to Italy for the summer whether I liked it or not. And the answer was not. I kicked a rock down the sidewalk in front of me. Today was the last day of my junior year of high school, and I was miserable. This summer was supposed to be fun. Swimming. Sailing. Sunbathing. A summer job selling Italian ice outside of the aquarium with my two best friends, Claire and Johan.

But no. In a week, I'd be in Montepulciano. Not Rome. Not Venice. Not Florence. Montepulciano.

Monte *what*? Whoever heard of that town? The Etruscans, that's who. They founded it. My mother is a classics professor at The College of Charleston so she spends lots of time studying ancient Romans and Greeks and the people who came before them, like the Etruscans. My dad is an archaeologist. He's leading a dig outside of Montepulciano, which means he can't come see me this summer. I have to go to him. I'd been on these research gigs before. Sure, I'd be in Italy ... digging in the dirt.

"*Mom!*" I'd whined. "Do I have to go for the *entire* summer? Really?"

My mom had looked tired, with dark circles under her normally lively blue eyes. The spring humidity made her short blonde hair curl softly around her pixie-like face, but the animation I was used to seeing there was missing. I felt guilty for being such a self-centered jerk, but I couldn't help myself. I really, really didn't want to go.

"Listen, Katie," she'd said. "I know you're disappointed about not spending the summer with your friends. But it's important that you go to Italy this summer."

"I've been to Italy before," I'd said. "Why can't it be next summer? Or the next one? Why *this* summer?"

I caught up with the rock and gave it a particularly vicious kick, sending it skittering into the intersection in front of me. I watched as it bounced into the gutter in front of a run-down house with a "For Sale" sign in the front yard. A man in a long black coat stood on the front porch. He had his hand on the doorknob, but he turned as soon as he heard the rock hit the curb. Icy blue eyes met mine for a second before he slipped through the door.

Why was the guy wearing a long leather coat in Charleston in June? The temperature at 8 a.m. was about 80 degrees, and it was already so humid I was sweating standing still. And yet the guy was dressed like a spy from some ancient British movie. Weird.

Just then, the light changed and I crossed, eager to get to school. I forgot about the man and his unseasonal attire as soon as I spotted Claire waiting for me in front of our high school.

Claire and I had plans to go shopping this afternoon. Not that I was happy about the reason we were going—I was supposed to be shopping for the trip to Italy.

"Hey! I want a pair of white sandals, and my mom gave me money so we can both get a pedicure this afternoon, too," Claire said, bouncing on her toes. "I'd really love bright red, but my mom says pink is better for spring. What do you think?"

I smiled, taking in Claire's energy. She was always like this—bouncy, energetic, up for anything. "I think we should go with pink to match the azaleas. Maybe we can get red later this summer, once we have a tan …" my voice trailed off as I realized I wouldn't be here later this summer.

"It's okay, Katie," Claire said. "You paint your toenails red in Italy and I'll paint mine red here, and we'll post the pictures on Instagram."

"It won't be the same," I said.

"No, it won't, but it's just for the summer," she said. "Just two and a half months. Ten weeks. Seventy days. But who's counting?"

I laughed, cheered up by the thought Claire would miss me, too.

Mrs. Mills, our homeroom teacher, was waiting by the door as we entered the classroom. She was holding a list of student names and a red pen.

"Books not turned in will have to be found by the end of the day or paid for," she said in her no-nonsense voice, looking at us over the top of her reading glasses. "Katie? Do you have all of your books?"

Claire and I turned in our books, watching anxiously as red check marks filled all the appropriate squares. We sat down in our seats to wait as other students trickled in—some with books and some with excuses. Johan stood in front of Mrs. Mills, his voice rising as he insisted that a book had been in his backpack the day before, and he knew he hadn't taken it out.

"Go check your locker again, Johan," she said. "Here. I'll write you a hall pass."

Johan, red-faced, stalked out of the room to look again.

"I wonder what he lost," Claire whispered. I shrugged back at her.

"Hey, I need to talk to you about something," I whispered back. "Last night after you left, I got an email from my dad. He said he wants to explain my 'heritage' to me, and that's why I'm going to Italy this summer. I mean, really. Does he think I don't know I'm half-Italian?"

A strange look passed over Claire's face and was gone so quickly I almost thought I'd imagined it. But the grimness in her voice was real enough.

"Katie," she said, taking a deep breath. "What exactly did the email say?"

"Here," I said, pulling the email up on my phone and handing it to her.

> Katie—
> I'm happy you'll be spending the summer helping me at the excavation site. It's time you learn about your heritage. There's much

you don't know, and it's time you
learn about it.

Love, Dad

Last night, I had stared at the message for a full minute, trying to figure out what he was talking about. Seriously, Dad? I knew I was half-Italian. We'd spent summers in Italy when my grandparents were still alive, before my parents' divorce. I spoke enough Italian to get by.

Claire's fair skin was paler than usual, but her tone was normal when she spoke again.

"Maybe he's found something related to your family at his dig," she said, handing my cell phone back to me.

"Whatever," I said, shrugging. I shoved the phone back into my backpack. I really wasn't interested in any more ancient history, and I had no idea what the Etruscans could possibly have to do with me. Just then, Johan returned. He spoke to Mrs. Mills in a low voice and took his seat. He was empty-handed, and he looked upset.

"What'd you lose?" I asked him.

"A library book," he said. "I put it in my backpack last night, but it's not there now. And it's a really old book; one that's not supposed to leave the library. Miss Bell let me take it home yesterday if I promised to return it today."

"What's it about?" I asked.

"History," he said, shrugging.

I raised my eyebrows.

The bell rang, and I swallowed my next question as Mrs. Mills gave me a stern glare. While Mrs. Mills called roll, I wondered about the real reason Johan had taken home a restricted book the day before school ended. I mean, if it'd been on sailing I'd understand ... but history? History of what?

"Okay, students," Mrs. Mills called out. "Let's all walk quietly to the gym."

We were having an awards ceremony for underclassmen. Seniors would be recognized at graduation on Saturday, but students in the lower grades would get their awards today. Johan stopped at his locker to check for the book again.

"Johan!" I hissed. "Move it! Mrs. Mills will notice if we're late!"

Suddenly, I saw the hem of a long black coat disappear around the corner to my left. It only took me two steps to get there, but the hall was empty.

"There's no need to run, Katie," Johan said. "I didn't take that long."

"Sorry," I replied absently, wondering if the guy in the black coat was now wandering the halls of our school. That was crazy. I shook my head. I must have imagined it. Claire gave me a strange look but didn't comment. The hum of excited voices echoed off the rafters and flowed around us as we settled on the bleachers in the gym.

I turned toward Johan and asked him, "So why'd you really check out that book?"

"I just wanted to get a head start on my senior thesis," he said.

"Seriously, Johan. How much research could you do when you only had the book for twenty-four hours?"

"Well," he squirmed, obviously not wanting to answer. I narrowed my eyes at him. I had all day. Or at least the next hour. He was trapped on the bleachers with nowhere to go.

"Enough," he said. "Only one chapter was important."

"Which one?"

"I'm researching some family history."

"You wouldn't be related to any ancient Etruscans, would you?" I asked. "Because I can help with that."

"That's part of the reason—" he paused as the principal called Claire's name. We were silent as Claire squeezed past us.

"Part of the reason what?"

"Katie, there's something I really need to talk to you about," Johan said.

"Emily Katherine Fiero."

It was my turn to head down to the floor. I smiled at Dr. Puckett, shook his extended hand, and took my award.

"Holly Rebekah Hill." I passed Holly as I headed back up the bleachers. Holly was a math whiz, so no surprise she'd won that award.

"What?" I asked, taking in the look on Johan's face as I sat back down. "Are you surprised I got the English award? You've got to let me beat you at something."

"No," he said. "You deserve it. I'm worried about you going to Montepulciano. It's not safe."

"Johan," I said. "That's ridiculous. It's a dusty Italian town where nothing ever happens."

"Katie," he said, running his hand through his light brown hair, his brows drawn down over his sea green eyes. "You can't go."

"Believe me, I've tried to talk my mom out of it. But my mom wants me to spend some time with my dad since I haven't seen him in so long. So I'm going. But we can Skype," I said brightly, wondering about his sudden concern for my safety.

"Johan Edward Meyer Jr."

I frowned as Johan headed down the bleachers to accept the history award. What was he so worried about? Really, it's not like I was going by myself. I'd be with my dad, supervised at all times. Although, now that I thought about it, this would be the first summer since we were born that Johan and I hadn't celebrated our birthdays together. Ah, the benefits of having birthdays a week apart and mothers who were best friends.

"So ... are you worried about turning seventeen without me? Afraid it won't happen if I'm not here?" I asked teasingly as Johan returned.

"No, it's not that," he said, turning red. "It's ... oh, never mind."

Johan turned back toward the front of the gym, and I realized the last award had been handed out. As we stood and headed down the bleachers, I tried to figure out what really had Johan so upset. I was pretty sure spending a boring summer helping my dad with his work didn't deserve that kind of concern.

CHAPTER TWO

2

The halls were crowded with students laughing and talking as we headed back to our classroom. Johan stopped so suddenly I slammed into him, and Claire barely kept herself from knocking us both over.

"What're you doing?" I hissed as I grabbed Claire's arm to steady myself. But then I saw what Johan was looking at. The door to his locker had been twisted off, the lock still intact. Papers were strewn all over the floor. Pencils and pens lay crushed as if a giant boulder had rolled down the hall. Mrs. Mills stood beside the mess, hands on her hips, glaring at us.

"Did you do this to cover up the fact that you can't find the book, Johan?" she demanded.

"No, ma'am. I was in the gym the entire time," he stuttered. "Ask Katie. She was right beside me."

"That's right," I said, looking at the twisted metal. "Besides, no offense, but I don't think Johan's strong enough to do that."

Johan started to say something, then stopped as Mrs. Mills narrowed her eyes and pressed her lips together, then waved us past.

"I'll speak to the principal and see what we should do about this," she said.

Johan, looking even paler than he had in the gym, took my arm as we entered the classroom.

"Katie, I don't know what's going on, but I think it has something to do with that book," he said in a low voice. "I'm going to go home and make sure it's not there. I'm a little worried."

"Can't you wait until school's out? It's only fifteen minutes," I said.

"No, I've got to go now. Cover for me," he said as he slipped into the hall.

I stared after him, wondering what I was supposed to say. Because, hello, Mrs. Mills wasn't an idiot. It was pretty much guaranteed she would notice he was gone. And sure enough, here she came, marching toward me with a severe look on her face.

"Where's Johan?"

I stared at her, my mind blank.

"He, um, was upset about his locker so he went to see Principal Puckett," Claire said.

I threw Claire a look of thanks as Mrs. Mills said, "Good, because that's where I was sending him."

She turned away from us and clapped her hands. "Now class, sit down and be quiet. We have just enough time to finish turning in books before the bell rings."

As Mrs. Mills called out names, Claire leaned toward me and hissed, "What's going on?"

"I don't know," I whispered back. "But I think Johan's in some kind of trouble. Something to do with an old book. When the bell rings, we need to go straight to his house."

She nodded and sat up straight as Mrs. Mills threw us a sharp look. My feet danced under my desk as I watched the clock tick off the last few minutes of my junior year. As the final bell began to clang, a cheer went up from the direction of the seniors' homeroom. Claire and I made our way quickly through groups of students hugging, exchanging phone numbers, and promising to stay in touch forever no matter what.

Claire and I broke into a trot as we reached the sidewalk and turned toward home. I live on Elizabeth Street, and Johan lives around the corner on Mary Street. Moving fast, it would take us about ten minutes to get there.

As we reached the head of Mary Street, we slowed to a walk. Oak trees draped in Spanish moss shaded the yards and sidewalks. Johan's neighbor, old Mrs. Ellis, watered the brightly-colored zinnias that grew in front of her house. A couple consulted a guidebook before heading toward East Bay Street and the shops and restaurants there. I heard the clip-clop of horses' hooves as a carriage full of tourists listened to the driver's patter of history mixed with jokes.

"Come on," I said to Claire.

As we got closer to Johan's house, I could see the front door was wide open. That wasn't right. Nobody in Charleston keeps their doors open in the summertime. Air conditioning can only do so much. I put my hand out, warning Claire. We went up the front steps and across the porch as quietly as we could, given that the house was more than two hundred years old and the boards creaked with every step.

Cool air blew out of the open door into our faces. We could hear the hum of the air conditioning unit as it struggled to keep up with the hot, humid air that was pouring in from the porch. The house was silent.

"Johan!" I called. "Are you here?"

No answer. We walked into the foyer, closing the door behind us. The house was a mirror image of mine. Stairs ran up the wall on the right to bedrooms upstairs. A hall straight ahead led toward the kitchen at the back of the house, and double doors opened onto a parlor on our left. The ceiling was high, and the wide pine boards of the floor gleamed with wax. Looking down the hall, I could see the back door was open, too. As I took a step toward the open door, I caught a glimpse of a long black coat in the backyard. That guy again? This time I was going to catch him.

I broke into a run, bursting into the backyard in time to see the tall blond man exit Johan's yard through the rear gate. He looked back at me, then took off in the same direction the tourists had gone. Like he was really going to blend in with all the people in tank tops and shorts wandering around down there. I was about to follow him when I heard a groan coming from the bushes on my left. Johan was lying in the dirt, his arm bent at a strange angle.

"Claire, call 911!" I yelled as I knelt beside him. "Johan, what happened?" I asked, taking off my empty backpack and folding it under his head.

"I'm not sure," he answered, taking a deep breath. "When I got here the front door was open.

There was nobody downstairs, so I went upstairs. I heard a noise in my room."

Johan paused to breathe, wincing as he tried to straighten his arm. Claire came out carrying a bag of ice and a can of tomato juice. She placed the ice on Johan's arm and helped him sit up enough to take a sip of juice.

"Why didn't you call the police as soon as you got here?" I asked.

"Well, um, I thought I knew who it was," he said.

"And did you?"

"Not really."

I waited, expecting him to go on. But he was silent. Finally, he looked at Claire.

"Did you call 911?" he asked.

"No."

"Good," he said.

"*What*? Why not?" I cried. "Your arm ..." My voice trailed off as I realized Johan was moving his arm normally, if a bit stiffly. It wasn't bent the wrong way anymore.

3

"Wait. What's happening?" I said, looking from Johan's face to Claire's, my eyes wide. "Johan's arm was broken. I saw it." My two best friends exchanged a look.

"It's time to tell her," Claire said. "She needs to know before she goes to Italy."

Great. Now my two best friends were keeping secrets from me. Between my dad's strange email and Johan's vague answers about the book, I was fed up.

"Come on, guys," I said. "This isn't funny."

"Yeah, you start," Johan said to Claire as he pushed himself into a sitting position. I gave Claire a hard look.

"Tell me what?" I asked. Claire smiled.

"Katie, I'm not a seventeen-year-old girl," she said.

I sat there for a minute, trying to make sense of that.

"Then what are you?" I asked, wondering what kind of joke they were trying to pull. "I mean, I've known you since we were ten."

"I'm a Garda," Claire said. I stared at her.

"And that means?"

"Literally?" she said. "Protector, guard. But I am specifically your protector. And that's why I showed up when your dad moved out."

I took a deep breath.

"So my dad knows who—what you are. Wait. He asked a ten-year-old girl to protect me?"

She nodded.

Maybe this is what the cryptic email I'd gotten last night was referring to. But what did Claire's being a Garda have to do with my own heritage? Unless maybe my heritage was why I needed a protector?

I was ten when my mom and dad divorced. My dad is Italian. He was a visiting professor at the College of Charleston one semester, and they fell madly in love. They fell just as madly out of love eleven years later. Grown-ups. Don't ask me to explain it, because I don't understand it myself. Anyway, he stayed on in Charleston after the split, at least until last year when he got an offer to lead the dig outside of Montepulciano.

I shook my head to clear it and fired more questions at Claire.

"And you were supposed to protect me? From what?" I asked, my voice rising.

"I told you, I'm not really a seventeen-year-old girl. And I wasn't a ten-year-old girl seven years ago. I am hundreds of years old, and can take any form necessary to protect you."

"You didn't answer the second part of the question. What are you protecting me from?"

Claire sighed. "That's a little more complicated."

"I'll try to explain," Johan said. "Let's start with me. I'm a vampire."

Now I knew for sure that either they were crazy or trying to play some kind of unfunny joke.

"So how are you sitting here in daylight? And why aren't you attacking me? And why don't you have pale skin and red eyes?" I would have kept going, but Johan held up his hand.

"Some of the things you've heard about vampires are true and some aren't," he said.

"For instance?"

"For instance, vampires are nocturnal, like owls. We see better in the dark. We prefer to hunt at night and sleep by day. However, like owls, we can change our routines if we need to. The sun doesn't hurt us. We can survive on animal blood—although human blood tastes better. And as you can tell, we look just like you. We do, however, heal faster than the average person," he said, flexing his arm.

"I've never seen you drinking blood."

I mean, yeah, it's not like I paid close attention to Johan's diet, but surely I would have noticed something like that.

"Katie," Johan said patiently. "Do you really think I drink tomato juice all the time?"

I stared at him. Johan didn't drink sodas. He drank tomato juice and said he did it because it was healthy and part of his training for the track team.

"You mean …"

"Yeah. It's not tomato juice."

Yuck.

"But what about your parents?"

"They're vampires, too. Duh. How do you think I got here?"

"I thought vampires couldn't have children."

"That's mostly true," Johan said, shrugging. "But every so often, say every five hundred years or so, a vampire couple has a child."

"Really?"

I think of more questions but decide I don't want to know that much about Johan's parents' sex life.

"What about the biting part?"

"Vampires can be made that way. A vampire will sometimes change a human companion so they're both vampires."

"So what happens if the human doesn't want to be a vampire?"

"Usually, they eventually break up," he said, pausing and looking at Claire.

She gave a slight nod. Johan took a deep breath and then continued, "Like your parents."

Okay, this was getting way too weird.

"What do you mean, like my parents? Yes, my parents broke up. But one of them isn't ..."

I stopped speaking as the expressions on their faces sank in. They were serious. They meant it. Oh, yeah. Guess Dad and I really were going to have a talk when I got to Italy. My voice wouldn't work. I cleared my throat and then whispered, "Which one?"

But I already knew. My mom was a morning person. She hopped out of bed at the break of dawn, singing and opening curtains to let in as much light as possible. My dad stayed up late reading, writing, studying. He always taught afternoon classes and worked through the night at excavation sites.

"So my mom didn't want to become a vampire?" I whispered.

"No. And she didn't want you to become one, either," Johan said gravely.

I looked at him in horror. "Me? What does this have to do with me?"

"Katie," he said gently. "You're half-vampire."

"But I don't have fangs. I don't stay up all night—at least not more than any other teenager. I don't drink blood! I don't even want to drink blood! What are you talking about?"

Johan sighed. "Okay, here it is. As the child of a human and a vampire, you have to make a choice. Once you reach seventeen, you can choose to stay human or become a vampire."

I'd reached my limit. I stood up and headed for home at a flat-out sprint, as though I could outrun the things Johan and Claire had just told me. When I reached my front door, I looked back. Claire and Johan hadn't followed me. I didn't see the man in the black coat, either. Uh-oh. I'd been so surprised that I hadn't even asked about him. I didn't know why he'd been in Johan's house or how Johan had ended up with a broken arm. Was the man a vampire? Something else? What else was there?

My thoughts ran in circles as I unlocked the front door and let myself in. It was 2:30. My mom would be home in an hour. I locked the door behind me, wishing we had a dog. A big, loud dog with sharp teeth. One that would let me know if a stranger were within a block of our house. Instead, Willow, my cat, wound herself around my ankles, meowing for me to put some food in her bowl. I closed my eyes and took a deep breath, then walked to the kitchen and filled her dish. She twitched her gray tail as she settled down to eat. If black-coat guy showed up, maybe she could purr him to death.

I flopped down in a kitchen chair, trying not to think about what Claire and Johan had told me. I just wanted to go back to this morning when I was a normal teenage girl with normal teenage friends, looking forward to a (somewhat) normal teenage summer. But no. My not-so-normal friends had to spoil everything.

Gradually, I realized I was hungry. I got up and rummaged through the refrigerator, looking for something that didn't take too much preparation. I finally settled on a cheese sandwich, stuck in the toaster oven for a minute or two so it kind of tasted like grilled cheese. Close enough, anyway.

As I ate, I tried to organize my thoughts. What about Claire's parents? Hadn't they noticed when Claire just suddenly showed up? Or were they, possibly, part of this, too? How much did my mom know? Why didn't Johan think I should go to Italy this summer? And I still didn't know why I needed protection.

I heard my mom's key turn in the front door. I wasn't ready to talk about this yet. I headed up the narrow back stairs, which took me straight from the kitchen to the hallway right outside of my room. Once inside, I closed the door and took out my cell phone. Now that I was calmer, I needed to talk to Claire.

CHAPTER FOUR

4

I sat on my bed and took a deep breath. I sent Claire a text: *Sorry I freaked. Come over?*

In a second, my phone rang.

"Katie, are you okay?" Claire asked.

"As okay as anyone could expect me to be," I said. "But I have some questions, and I'm not ready to talk to my mom about this."

"Right. And we still need to go shoe shopping," Claire said. "I'll be right over."

Really? How could she think about shoes when I'd just found out I was half-vampire and some crazy guy in a black coat was running around tearing the doors off lockers and breaking people's arms? Okay, one locker and one arm. Still, shoes?

"Katie?"

It was my mom. I checked myself in the mirror. Amazing. I still looked like the same girl who'd left for school this morning. I ran a comb through my hair, surprised that I looked so normal, and answered.

"Yeah, Mom?"

"Did you get your shoes yet?" she asked, opening the door to my bedroom. She came in and sat down on the edge of my bed. Wow. She was thinking about shoes, too.

"Not yet. Claire's on her way over now," I said.

"Okay. I'm going to take a shower and grade some papers," Mom said, getting up and heading for her room. "We'll eat supper when you get back. Claire's welcome to stay if she wants."

"Thanks, Mom. I'll tell her."

As I headed downstairs, I realized I'd left my backpack at Johan's, and my wallet was in it. Just then, the doorbell rang. Claire stood there with my backpack in her hand. She thought of everything. I guess that was part of her job, though, as a protector. Huh. No wonder she was always so organized. She'd had centuries to get it together. So not fair.

I opened the door and stepped out. I pulled my wallet out of the backpack, tucking it into the purse I'd slung over my shoulder. I tossed the backpack inside, locking the door behind me.

"First, is my mom safe?" I asked.

"Not so loud," Claire said in a low voice, looking around. "But don't worry. My parents take turns keeping watch over her. She's as safe as you are."

"Well, that answers one of my questions," I said. "So your parents are, um, protectors, too?"

"Garda," she said. "Yes, they are. And they're not really my parents. I'm as old as they are."

I took a minute to think about that. So Claire hadn't just appeared in some unsuspecting couple's house at age ten and made herself at home. And if Claire was hundreds of years old, then her "parents"... okay, next subject.

"Exactly why do we need protection? You haven't explained that part."

"You did run off a little abruptly."

"Yeah, well, I needed to think."

"You've absorbed a lot today, but to answer your question, your dad is not just any vampire. He's a Stregoni Benefici."

"A what?" I asked.

"Stregoni Benefici," Claire repeated slowly. "Literally translated, it means beneficent wizard. What that means to you is he's a member of a vampire branch that works to protect humans from creatures that would harm them, including other vampires.

"Not all vampires want to live among humans, feeding from animals and adjusting their schedules away from the nocturnal. There are some who would like to return to the days when monsters ruled the world, when humans were afraid to go outside from dusk to daybreak, and people who traveled at night often disappeared."

"Well," I said hesitantly, "that's good, right? I mean, good that my dad wants to keep people safe."

"It is," Claire said. "But some of the other vampires have decided to focus their efforts on removing the Stregoni Benefici, or at least limiting their numbers. And you have the capability to turn into one."

I felt the gears in my head lock up. I slowed my steps as we neared our destination, the Bob Ellis shoe store on King Street. I cleared my throat, trying to get my brain to work again.

"You mean … I'm supposed to grow up to fight bad vampires?" I said. "And by 'removing' the Strego whatever, you mean 'kill,' right?"

It sounded so ridiculous said out loud like that. I was supposed to grow up to be a professor, like my mom and dad. They were both passionate about the subjects they taught, and loved bringing the past alive for their students. I'd always planned on following in their footsteps. I couldn't possibly fight vampires *and* teach, could I? But then I realized that my dad, if he really was a vampire warrior, was a professor as well. Apparently it was possible to do both. As if teaching classes and doing research weren't enough to keep you busy. Claire nodded calmly, opening the door to the shoe store.

"Come on, Katie, let's find some sandals," she said.

What was it with these people and shoes?

CHAPTER FIVE

We walked out thirty minutes later with shoeboxes swinging from our hands. We'd each bought a pair of strappy sandals, perfect to offset summer tans. We'd also bought espadrilles—very retro, but very cool, too. And perfect for Italy. Which reminded me.

"How much does my mom know?" I asked Claire.

"You'll need to talk to her about that. But Johan and I thought you should know the truth before you leave for Italy."

"What do you mean? What's wrong with Italy?"

"It's too dangerous. While Montepulciano is where the Stregonis live, only a few meters away is Volterra, home of the Velathri."

I stared at her.

"So ... the Vel, um, Velathri, are evil?"

"Well ..." Claire hesitated. "Let's just say they're traditionalists. There's some history you need to know. And then we need to go talk to your mom."

"My mom? I'm not ready to discuss this with her! I'm not sure I believe it myself!"

"I know. But by insisting on taking you to Italy, she's set something in motion, and we have to figure out what."

"Set something in motion ... you mean black-coat guy?"

Claire stared at me.

"You saw him?" she asked.

"Yes, of course I saw him," I said. "Three times today."

"Three times? When?"

"This morning on the way to school, at school right before the door was ripped off of Johan's locker, and then at Johan's house," I said. "Is he the one who hurt Johan?"

"Johan can tell you that," Claire said, not meeting my eyes. "Let's go to my house. I have something to show you."

I could tell Claire wasn't going to answer my question. Fine. I'd ask Johan when I saw him. I was going to get to the bottom of this, one way or the other.

Claire led the way to her house, around the corner from mine on Chapel Street. Her parents weren't home from work yet, so we went straight to her room. I looked around, wondering how an ancient being's room could look so much like a teenage girl's. Her bed was rumpled and unmade, and dirty clothes filled the hamper, trailing onto the floor.

"So why are those other vampires called Velathri?" I asked.

Claire was digging in the back of her closet. In a muffled voice she said, "Because that's the original name of Volterra—the name the Etruscans gave the city when they founded it."

Those stupid Etruscans again. It was their fault my summer had been ruined. How could a civilization that ended thousands of years ago still be causing so much trouble?

Claire backed out of her closet, clutching what looked like an old leather-bound guide book in her hand. She opened it to a map of Italy, and handed it to me.

"What's this?" I asked, examining the map.

"Look closely. The names aren't place names—they're family names. Different vampire families control different areas of the world. The oldest families are in Italy. For centuries, the Velathri have pretty much overseen the entire vampire world. Nobody voted; it just kind of evolved that way. They had the power; they used it. But about a hundred years ago, technology began changing the way humans, and other beings, interacted with each other. The automobile, the airplane, the internet, cell phones, Skype—it's much easier to visit and stay in touch with other areas of the world than it used to be."

I nodded, understanding the technology part, but wondering how it affected vampire politics.

"There have always been half-vampires, and the Velathri have always disapproved. But families used to simply leave Italy. They'd move to another part of Europe, or take a ship to the United States or Canada. Some even settled in Australia and New Zealand. And the Velathri were fine with that. But now, their influence is wider. And they're purists. They don't like half-vampires—children who may or may not know about them, children who may or may not grow up to be vampires themselves. How much these children know, how much they'll reveal to the rest of the world, and what they'll do when they reach seventeen is unpredictable. And the Velathri don't like unpredictability. They like certainty. They like control."

I suddenly remembered the man in the black coat. "So who's the guy in the black coat? Is he a Velathri?" I asked.

"Maybe. I didn't get a close enough look at him," Claire said.

Her voice sounded odd, but she was looking down at the book, and I couldn't read her expression. My mind skipped back to the book in my hand.

"So this book is what, exactly?" I asked.

"It's a history of vampires," Claire said.

"And what about the book Johan had?"

"It's a history of the Tuatha de Danann."

"The Two-who?"

"I'm Garda. The Tuatha are our cousins who, I guess you could say, are traditionalists like the Velathri," Claire said. "They live hidden, in caves and underground, avoiding contact with humans."

"How is that even possible?"

"It's becoming more and more difficult," Claire replied.

"So ... why was the book in our school library?"

"Your dad put it there. The librarian thinks it's an old book on Irish history, and it is, I guess. Your dad didn't think it would be safe in Europe, and he wanted you to be able to read it when you were old enough. And he thought the reference section of a high school library would be a safe hiding place," Claire said.

"Ireland? Irish history? I thought we were talking about Italy and vampires," I said, confused.

She closed her eyes and sighed. "The seat of vampire power is in Italy—Volterra. The seat of fairy power is in Ireland …"

"*Fairy* power? When did we start talking about fairies?" I yelled, startling Claire into opening her eyes.

"Garda and Tuatha are fairies," she said. "I thought you understood that."

"*No!*" I shouted. "How was I supposed to know that?"

Claire sighed. "I'm trying to explain, but your parents have made it hard by letting you think you were human all these years."

"Well, I'm really sorry to inconvenience you," I said through gritted teeth. "But we are talking about my *entire life* here."

"I think I'll let your mother take it from here," Claire said. "Let's go back to the book Johan lost. It's the companion book to this one." She pointed to the book I held. "Your dad found them on one of his digs. There's supposed to be a third one, but your dad hasn't been able to find it."

"Why do the Velathri want the books? Don't they know their own history?"

"Yes, but as I said, they like control. And having the books gives them power."

I thought about the implications of what she'd just said. "Control over …"

"Well, vampires they don't like. Garda, like me. And all the other creatures listed in the books—witches, wizards, werewolves, trolls, giants …"

I held up my hand. "Stop," I said. "You mean …"

But of course. If vampires really existed, then the other creatures had to as well. I closed my eyes and took a deep breath. I felt like the earth was crumbling under my feet. The world as I had thought it existed was a lie. Instead, a hidden world of danger and legend had been going on around me while I contemplated what color nail polish would look best. I decided to worry about what else was out there later.

"So does black-coat guy have the other book?"

"We don't think so, because why tear up Johan's locker and search Johan's house if he's got it? But Johan doesn't know what happened to it, and that's bad."

"Why did Johan take it out of the library anyway?" I asked.

Claire sighed. "He wasn't supposed to. Your dad had a witch place a spell on the book, to make sure it didn't fall into the wrong hands."

"A witch? A spell?"

"Yes, Katie," Claire said patiently. "The books were lost for a long time. Everyone thought all three of them were destroyed when Mt. Vesuvius buried Pompeii. But apparently some enterprising vampires snuck them out, at least the two your dad has found, and hid them. Your dad found the first one, the one you're holding, about twenty years ago. It was hidden in a Catholic monastery outside of Rome. He found the other one a year ago, in a grotto in Ireland. When your dad came to visit last fall, he put it in the school library."

"How did you get this one?"

"Your dad gave it to me so I could show it to you when the time was right. And where better to hide something than in the back of a teenage girl's closet, under clothes and shoes and pocketbooks?"

I laughed.

"Yeah, even my mother the neat freak would probably leave that alone," I said. I sobered at the thought of my mother. "We need to talk to her, don't we?" I asked.

"Yep," Claire said. "Maybe we can find out why she's so determined to send you to Italy this summer."

"Oh, I forgot! She invited you for supper."

"Perfect," Claire said. "Let's get moving."

Claire buried the book in the back of her closet again, arranging clothing so the floor of her closet looked like a perfectly random mess.

I grabbed my Bob Ellis shopping bag, and we headed for my house. As we walked, another thought occurred to me. "Do the Velathri know you have one of the books?" I asked.

"No and neither does Johan. So don't say anything," Claire said. "If the Velathri knew they were both in Charleston, they would double their efforts to find them."

I felt like I'd aged about ten years in the past ten hours. Not only was there a whole other world out there, but it was on the verge of a war over two books my dad had unearthed.

"Um … I get the feeling my dad's pretty important in all of this," I said.

"Yes, he is," Claire said. "Not every half-vampire gets her own personal Garda."

I shook my head. "This feels really … unreal."

"I know," Claire agreed. "And I'm sorry you had to find out like this. Usually, children are taught these things little by little as they grow up, and have years to absorb what you've just learned today. But your parents had their reasons for keeping you in the dark."

As we walked up the front steps, my mom threw open the front door.

"Katie, Claire!" She exclaimed. "You're okay!"

As my mother threw her arms around me, I saw Johan and his parents, Edward and Juliana Meyer, standing in our parlor. Johan looked like his dad—light brown hair, green eyes, a dusting of freckles across his nose. His dad's hair was shorter than Johan's, and he wore a pair of wire-rim glasses, but that was about the only difference. He was the image of a forgetful college professor, but I guess that, like everything else, was a lie or only partially true.

Mrs. Meyer was beautiful. Her smooth dark hair was pulled into an elegant chignon. She wore a red dress that showed off her tan skin, brown eyes, and matching red lipstick. I looked at these people with new eyes, trying to fit my years of knowing them as simply my friend's parents with what I had learned earlier that day.

"Of course we're okay," Claire said. "What's happened?"

"Johan told us the book is missing," Mr. Meyer said. "This is serious, and we need to talk about it. Your parents are on the way over, Claire."

My mom didn't seem surprised at all.

"Let's go into the kitchen," she said. "I've got supper ready."

Mom had prepared a huge pot of spaghetti, salad, and a platter full of garlic bread. Had she known there would be more than three of us? It certainly looked like it. I shot her a look, but she was busy setting the table and didn't meet my eyes.

"Let's go ahead and start," Mom said. "The Corbetts can join us when they get here."

We sat down and filled our plates. The room was quiet for a few minutes as we all ate. Every person at the table seemed familiar with the European custom of twirling noodles with spoon and fork. Huh, I'd never noticed that before. I was pretty sure my other American friends didn't eat pasta that way. In fact, my friend Bethany's mom didn't even put out spoons when she served spaghetti. I'd always assumed my mom had picked up the custom from my dad. I snuck another look at my mom, but she kept her eyes on her plate. She stood up to get the door when Claire's parents arrived, still not looking my way.

"Bonjour, Katherine," Mrs. Corbett said, nodding at me.

"Hi," I said. I never really knew what to make of her. She always greeted me in French, and used my given name, even though everyone else calls me Katie.

"This is wonderful, Libby," Adam said, sitting down to a heaping plate of spaghetti. "I really miss authentic Italian cooking. Ariel has never mastered it, despite our years in Montepulciano."

"No, I am French," Ariel said. "The cooking I do is superior."

So these guys had apparently been in Italy together. I wondered when. I looked over at my mother again. She looked the other way, pretending she didn't notice me trying to imitate the death stare she'd used on me when I was younger. I stood up and started cleaning the kitchen as the Corbetts ate. Claire and Johan pitched in. I was full of nervous energy, wondering what other surprises I was in for.

When we were all seated at the table again, Mr. Corbett cleared his throat and looked at Claire, who began describing our day. When she got to the part about black-coat guy at Johan's house, she stopped for a second, and then said, "Katie saw him three times today."

"Where, Katie?" Mr. Corbett said. "What was he doing?"

"I saw that guy this morning, on my way to school," I said. I described seeing him enter the house near the school, while I waited for the light to change. "And I thought I saw him in the school while we were on the way to the gym," I added.

Everyone at the table stared at me.

"What?" I asked. I looked down at the front of my shirt, checking for spaghetti splotches.

"You shouldn't be able to see this man," Mr. Meyer said, wrinkling his forehead. "Supernatural creatures are able to hide their movements from humans."

"Actually, Katherine is unique," Mrs. Corbett said, studying me as though I were a bug under a microscope. "Vampire-fairy children are rare. We do not know what will happen when she turns seventeen."

Okay. She'd said vampire-fairy, not vampire-human. I looked around the table. The Meyers—Edward, Juliana, and Johan—were vampires. The Corbetts—Adam, Ariel and Claire—were faries. And if I was half-vampire, half-fairy, and I knew my dad was a vampire, then that made my mom ... I looked at her. Her face was serious as she finally returned my gaze. My mom was an ancient being who protected others. An Irish fairy, if I believed Claire. I closed my eyes, feeling faint.

CHAPTER SIX

6

When I opened them again, I was lying on the floor. My mom held a cold washcloth on my forehead while Claire fanned me with a magazine.

"Ariel, you should have let Libby tell her," Claire hissed.

Claire had called her mother Ariel. Wait. I knew this. Ariel wasn't really her mother.

"I thought you told her this afternoon," Mrs. Corbett—Ariel—said, unconcerned. "Isn't that what you were supposed to be doing?"

"I only got to the vampire part. I was going to let her mother tell her the other part," Claire said in an exasperated voice.

I pushed myself into a sitting position.

"Let's just get on with it," I said, getting to my feet. "I'd like to know everything. Now."

"See? She is tougher than you think," Mrs. Corbett said, winking at me.

I wasn't sure I agreed with her methods, but at least I was finally getting the truth. I took my seat at the table, folding my hands in front of me while I waited for the others to sit back down. Johan sat beside me, looking as shocked as I felt. It occurred to me that maybe he hadn't known everything, either.

"I think it would be more efficient if we let Katie ask us questions as we don't know exactly what knowledge Claire was able to impart this afternoon," Mr. Meyer said, looking around the group. At their nods, he turned to me. "But to begin with, you should call us by our first names," he said.

I raised my eyebrows and looked at my mom. I'd been raised in the South, taught from birth that you call adults "Mr." and "Mrs." and definitely not by their first names.

"He's right, Katie," Mom said. "It's time. I've raised you to fit into this culture, but in our culture, where people live for centuries, we go by first names."

"So that's settled. Now, what would you like to know?" Mr. Meyer—Edward—said.

I tried to gather my thoughts. I looked around the table and took a deep breath.

"Okay. Let's start with all of you. How old is everyone?"

"We're all older than we look," Edward answered. "Vampires age, but very slowly. I am close to four hundred years old. Juliana is three hundred this year."

"What about Johan? We were babies together!"

"Babies are very rare among vampires. But Johan is really sixteen years old. Which is why he thought he could handle finding the book by himself," Edward said.

I looked at Johan, who had gone to nursery school with me. At least that much of my life had been real. Well, if you ignored the whole "he's a vampire" part.

"So what about the book?" I asked.

"I'm sorry," Johan said, looking at his dad. "I heard you and mom talking about the book, and how to get it from the library, and I thought I could help. Miss Bell likes me."

"But now the book is lost," Adam said gravely.

"Wait a minute," I said slowly. "Is it possible that black-coat guy is a Garda, not a Velathri?" I asked.

"Ah," Adam said. "What makes you think that?"

I looked from Adam to Ariel to Claire to my mom. Every single one of them was fair-skinned, blond and blue-eyed. "He had blond hair and blue eyes," I said. "He looked like all of you."

"Oh, she's quick, this one," Ariel said. "Yes, it is possible."

I looked down at my tanned arm, and thought of my brown eyes and dark hair. If I became a Garda when I turned seventeen, would I suddenly become blond and blue-eyed? But I had more pressing questions to ask.

"Why would he want the book? And why would he tear the door off of Johan's locker?"

"If he is Garda, then I don't think he tore the door off the locker," my mom said. "That sounds much more like the Velathri."

"Then why would he break Johan's arm?" I asked indignantly.

"Um, that wasn't him," Johan said.

"But I saw him leaving your backyard through the gate in the back corner," I said.

"Yeah, he was there. But he's the one who saved me. The other guy would have killed me if he hadn't shown up."

"What other guy?" I asked. I looked around. Apparently this wasn't news to anyone else.

"There was another guy at the house when I got there," Johan said. "Not a vampire. Something else, but still really strong. He was ... I don't know, ruthless. He picked me up and threw me out of my bedroom window like it was nothing. He was coming after me when the blond guy showed up, and they both took off."

"So who has the book?" I asked. "The Garda or the Velathri? Or someone else?"

There was a long silence. Finally, my mother spoke.

"We don't know," she said slowly. "It appears the Velathri are searching for it, which means they don't have it. Yet. As for where it is ..."

"That, we will attempt to find out tomorrow," Adam said. "We should rest. It's almost midnight, and tomorrow will be a busy day."

There went my two days of leisure between the last day of school on Wednesday and graduation on Saturday. Claire and I had never gotten pedicures. I had more shopping to do to get ready for a summer in Italy ... but it appeared those plans were on hold. Maybe forever.

"No, Adam," my mother said, looking at me. "She's too young."

"She's the same age as Johan," Juliana said.

"It's time to stop protecting her, Libby," Ariel said. "I know you wanted to wait, but events have been set in motion earlier than we expected."

"I need to let Anthony know what's happening," my mom said. Anthony is my dad.

"No, it's too dangerous," Adam replied. "Phones, email, texts can all be intercepted."

"I have already sent him a message through other channels," Edward said. "It's slower than modern technology, but safer. He should get it by tomorrow."

My mom sighed, but I could see she agreed.

"So why are we going to Italy if it's so dangerous?" I asked the question Claire had voiced earlier in the day.

"Because we don't know how your gifts will manifest themselves, your father thinks you should be in Montepulciano, home of the Stregoni Benefici," my mother said. "The books both contain information about vampire-fairy children, so we need them there as well."

"Somehow, the Velathri have been alerted," Adam said. "At least to the existence of the book Johan had. We hope they remain unaware of the other book, and of you."

"They don't know about me?" I asked. That made me feel a little better.

"More to the point, they don't know about your mother. They believe she is human, not Garda. So they think you are half-human, half-vampire, and that she intends to keep you in the dark about your heritage, so you will remain human. They're simply watching to be sure this is what happens. If they knew you were half-Garda, you would be in much more danger."

I sat in silence, absorbing what he had said. So my parents had kept this huge secret to keep me safe. But now, my dad wanted me in Italy.

"Why does Dad think I'll be safer in Italy?" I said.

"Because Montepulciano is the base of Stregoni Benefici power," Edward said. "Velathri can't enter without permission, just as we can't enter Volterra."

Well, that was interesting. And of course it was Montepulciano, not someplace cool like New York or London or Paris. I sighed.

"Claire can stay here tonight as extra protection for Katie," Edward said. "The rest of us should keep to our regular schedules."

Claire and I went upstairs and everyone else headed for home. We got ready for bed, not speaking.

Claire took the other twin bed in my room, like so many times before. I turned off the light, and looked over at the lump in the other bed that was Claire. It felt so normal—so much a part of my old life—to have her there. But everything was different. She wasn't really my age. She wasn't really my best friend—she was my protector. Her parents weren't really her parents.

My brain was so stuffed with new information, I was sure I'd never get to sleep. I had so many more questions. I yawned. I'd just close my eyes for a minute …

CHAPTER SEVEN

7

I woke up to find sunlight streaming through the window and the other bed empty. I took a quick shower and put on my favorite khaki shorts and a red T-shirt. I ran downstairs to find Johan and Claire sitting at the kitchen table. Willow was curled up in Johan's lap, purring.

"I thought vampires had to be invited in," I said, rubbing Willow's ears.

"We do," Johan said. "But everyone has to be invited in to your house, not just vampires."

I stared at him. "What do you mean?"

Claire cleared her throat. "You know those Celtic knots your mother collects?"

"Yeah," I said. "They're kind of a hobby of hers."

"More than a hobby," Claire said. "They have protective power. Have you ever wondered why the doorways to your house have carvings on the stone stoops?"

"No," I shrugged. "It's just something old. But everything in Charleston is old."

"Charleston is old for America, but it's just a baby compared to cities in Europe," Claire said. "The carved stones at your house came from Ireland and are thousands of years old. The specific carving is a triskelion. It's really important in Celtic legend. Ask your mother. She's done a lot of research and even published a few articles on it."

"Okay," I said, thinking Claire had been a lot more fun before I knew she was my protector.

"So what's happening today?"

"Your mom and Johan's parents have gone to work, because it would look suspicious if they didn't show up," Claire said, picking up her plate and putting it in the dishwasher. "Adam and Ariel are doing a little research to see if they can find out who might want to steal the book other than the Velathri."

"It feels strange to hear you call your parents Adam and Ariel," I said to Claire.

"Maybe to you, but they aren't my parents. Ariel has had too much fun bossing me around for the past seven years," Claire said.

"What about us?" I asked.

"We're supposed to do normal stuff. Not draw attention to ourselves," Johan said. "But we have to stick together."

"Okay. Claire and I were going to get pedicures," I said.

Johan groaned. "Like that'll look normal for me."

I laughed.

"We'll skip it since you're with us. What else can we do?" I asked as I pulled the Cheerios from the pantry.

I looked down at the yellow box in my hand. It was so normal, so reassuring. I remembered yesterday morning, eating Cheerios before I headed to school for the last day of my junior year. Wow, was that really just yesterday? If Johan and Claire weren't sitting in front of me I would think it was all a dream. Johan was drinking a can of tomato juice. I tried not to think about what that meant. I poured cereal and milk in a bowl, sliced a banana over the top, and began to eat, still staring at the can in Johan's hand.

"So, Johan," I said, clearing my throat. "You ate food last night. Do you need to?"

"No, blood is all I need," Johan said. "But I can eat."

"Yeah, I figured that out all on my own," I said, just a little snippily.

"I think we should walk around downtown," Claire interjected. "We can act like we're helping you shop for your trip to Italy while we watch for anything strange."

"Okay," Johan nodded. "I had an idea about the book. Maybe we can follow up on it."

"Nothing too dangerous. I may be a Garda, but there is only one of me," Claire said.

"Nah, it's not dangerous," he said. "There's a bookstore downtown. It sells used and antique books. What if someone stole the book out of my backpack, thinking it was just some old book they could sell for some extra money? I mean, I know it's not likely, but it's worth a try."

"That sounds safe enough," Claire said. "And it fits with our cover of shopping." She turned to me. "Katie, when you're ready, we'll go."

I finished my cereal and ran upstairs to brush my hair into a ponytail and put on my running shoes. I looked longingly at my new espadrilles. But a day walking around downtown Charleston, possibly being chased by mysterious guys in black coats? I decided comfort and speed were more important than style. I grabbed a small purse out of my closet, and added a brush, lip gloss, and a change purse with some cash in it. If I shopped with cash, I wouldn't need an ID, and I didn't want to unpack my regular wallet, which was already stashed in my carry-on bag, ready for the trip to Italy. I looped the narrow strap over my head and across my right shoulder, and ran down the stairs.

"Okay, I'm ready," I told Claire and Johan. The three of us headed out the front door. I locked it behind me, pushing aside the sudden unwelcome thought that a lock wasn't going to keep out the really dangerous things. I looked down at the three swirls carved into the stone at my feet. Was that really more powerful than a lock? Maybe Claire's talk this morning hadn't just been boring history stuff.

We walked toward King Street, taking the same route Claire and I had taken the day before.

"Let's walk toward the school," I said. "I'll show you the house I saw black-coat guy going into yesterday."

When we reached the intersection, I looked left. The "For Sale" sign was still out front, but there was no one on the front porch today.

Claire looked around with a worried expression on her face. "We should keep walking. Something feels wrong."

"No," Johan said. "I think we should take a look inside."

"Absolutely not," Claire said. "It's my job to protect the two of you. I'll call one of the others and have them search while we keep shopping."

"I just want to check for the book." Johan had a familiar stubborn set to his mouth. "I lost it. It's my responsibility to get it back."

He started toward the house, ignoring Claire's hissed, "Johan! No!" Claire and I started after him, but he'd already reached the front door. He tried it, rattling the doorknob, and when he found it locked, Johan shrugged and started around the house toward the back door.

"Johan! Stop!"

Again, he ignored Claire and disappeared behind the house. Claire looked at me. "Stay here."

I'd watched enough horror movies to know *that* was a bad idea.

"No way," I replied. "Do you really think I'm going to stand out here by myself? That's asking for trouble."

"I guess you're right," Claire sighed. "Come on."

I followed Claire as she walked carefully around the side of the house. The backyard was empty, and the back door was open. Claire and I shared an exasperated glance and followed Johan into the house. The back door opened into a kitchen that was obviously being used, even though the house looked unlived in from the street. Clean dishes were stacked in the drain rack. The stainless steel sink and faucets gleamed as the morning sun streamed in the window. I walked over to the pantry and opened the door. Basic staples were stocked—crackers, canned goods, bottled water. No tomato juice, I noticed.

Claire whipped around at the sound of footsteps, but it was just Johan coming down the stairs.

"There's nobody here," he said, disappointment in his voice.

"Well, that's a good thing," Claire said. "Any sign of the book?"

"I can't tell," he answered, his shoulders slumping. "The upstairs is a huge mess."

"Like the people who lived here were slobs or like someone was looking for something?" she asked.

"Come see for yourself."

The upstairs had been ransacked. Drawers had been pulled out and dumped, books pulled off the bookshelves and strewn around the room. Chairs lay on their sides. A side table had been crushed to splinters.

"Wow," I said. "Somebody was ticked off."

"If the book was here, it isn't now," Claire said grimly. "We need to leave. And don't go off by yourself like that again, Johan. The Velathri don't mess around."

We left quickly, closing the back door behind us. Claire looked around as we crossed the street, sniffing the air as she turned her head from side to side. Her movements were smooth, almost feline. How had I never noticed this about my best friend? Or was she just not hiding her true self anymore?

We passed our school on Calhoun Street. It already had that empty, lonely look schools have during summer vacation. As we walked, I decided to ask a few more questions.

"If I'm so special, why don't I feel special? Why don't I have superpowers?" I asked, partly joking, but mostly not.

"You do," Johan said.

"Like what?"

"Think about how fast you can run."

I was the fastest person on the track team except for Bryan Blalock, a sophomore.

"Bryan's faster than me," I said.

"I know," Johan said, giving me a half-smile.

"You mean …"

"Yep. Bryan's a vampire," Johan smiled.

I thought that over. Bryan liked tomato juice, too.

"So … is everyone who drinks tomato juice …"

Johan laughed. "No. Some people just like tomato juice. And it is healthy, if you're human. But no one at our school is human. At least, not completely."

"What do you mean?" I asked. "I'm human!"

"No, you're half-fairy and half-vampire. You've just been raised to believe you're human," Claire said. "Everyone in our school—teachers and students—has at least one supernatural parent."

"Why?" I sputtered.

"It's just safer that way," Claire said.

"So everyone knows about this? Except me?"

Johan shrugged. I took that as a yes. I was starting to get a little annoyed. Okay, a lot annoyed.

"What else should I know?"

"You heal as fast as I do," Johan said.

"How do you know? I've never had a bad injury," I said.

"But you should have, remember?" Johan said. "The time you fell off the monkey bars in first grade? And how about when you ran your bicycle into the side of a car in third grade? A moving car? And the time you fell out of a tree in sixth grade? Don't you think you should have broken a bone at least one of those times?"

I stopped walking, shocked by Johan's statements.

"I guess I never thought about it. The school nurse was pretty freaked out, though."

"Yeah, that's because your leg was broken, but by the time she splinted it and got you into her office, it was healed. She thought she was going crazy."

"I remember my mom wasn't too happy, either," I said.

"Right," Johan said. "She was afraid people would figure out you were different."

"And the next year she transferred me to St. Francis ..."

As I turned that over in my mind, we reached King Street and took a left, heading toward the market. Johan wasn't sure exactly where the bookstore was, but he said he knew it was near the shopping district.

A few blocks down, Johan stopped. "That's it," he said, pointing at a narrow storefront beside a coffee shop.

"Where?" I said. "I don't see a bookstore."

The building he pointed to was brick, with a glass door in a wooden frame and a large front window. There were a few books in the window, but none of them were on the New York Times Bestseller List. Some of them looked downright ancient—like pre-printing press ancient. A hand-lettered sign encouraged us to "Seek Shade." Not bad advice for June in Charleston, but still. This was the place we were looking for?

"Look at the door," Johan said.

Inside a small square, the name "Blue Bicycle Books" was painted on the glass.

"Blue Bicycle? What kind of name is that for a bookstore?" I asked.

"I don't know. I didn't name it," Johan said, shrugging. "Come on, let's go in."

"Wait," Claire said. "Something still doesn't feel right." She stood unmoving, her eyes closed.

"What are you doing?" I hissed.

"Quiet," she said. "I'm listening."

Finally, she opened her eyes. "I can't tell," she said, looking frustrated. "I think it's safe, but I'm not sure. Stay near me."

A bell chimed as we pushed open the door. A large orange cat napping on the counter raised its head and blinked at us sleepily. It purred as I scratched its ears.

All three of us jumped when a voice addressed us. "Are you looking for something in particular, or just browsing?"

A character from a Charles Dickens novel peered at us from the next room. He wore a pressed white shirt with a high collar. Suspenders held up his black trousers, and his eyes twinkled above thick mutton-chop whiskers that would have made Wolverine jealous.

"William," Claire said, sounding pleased. "I didn't know you were in Charleston."

As we walked toward him, I realized the store was much larger than it looked from outside. It was long and narrow, a series of rooms. Wooden ladders that slid along metal tracks let you climb up to reach books on the shelves near the ceiling. I didn't think I'd ever seen this many books crammed into such a small space in my life.

"Been here for decades, my dear," William said, smiling. "Who are your friends?"

Obviously, these two knew each other. My best friend was full of surprises today.

"This is Katie, my assignment," she said. "And this is Johan, her friend."

Huh? When did I go from a best friend to an assignment?

"I am pleased to meet you both," William said, bowing gravely. "What brings you to my shop?"

"Johan lost a book, and we were wondering if someone might have tried to sell it here," Claire said.

"When did you lose this book?" William said, turning to Johan.

"Yesterday," Johan said. "I had it Tuesday evening, but when I looked in my backpack Wednesday morning, it was gone."

"And what is the title?"

"*Rulers of Ireland*," Johan replied.

William went very still, his eyes the only movement as he looked at each of our faces in turn. Finally, he spoke.

"Yes, I have seen this book. But not here, and not in this century," he said cautiously.

"What do you mean, not in this century?" I asked.

"The last time I saw this book, it was in Rome in the year 1012. I owned a bookshop there, and someone sold it to me. If I saw it again, I would not buy it."

"Wait. Did you really just say 1012?" I stared at the man, trying to calculate how old that made him.

"Yes, of course," William replied, looking surprised.

Claire's elbow jabbed into my ribs. Right, I was supposed to know this stuff.

"So, um, why wouldn't you buy the book again," I said.

"Because it nearly cost me my life, my dear. My bookshop was burned by those seeking the book, and I spent centuries in hiding. Eventually, I made my way to the New World, and opened another bookshop here in Charles Towne. Now tell me. How did you come by this book?"

"My father found it excavating an archaeological site, and he hid it in our school library," I said. "But Johan checked it out and now it's gone."

"Best that it is lost again, my dear. That book is dangerous, and those who seek it even more so."

"No, William, we need to find it," Claire said gently. "We can't let it fall into the wrong hands."

"I'm just a merchant," William said. "I avoid politics. I want to live in peace and sell books."

"But if this book falls into the wrong hands, your peaceful life won't be allowed to continue," Claire said. "Those who seek this book would wipe out werewolves along with the rest of us."

My eyes widened. Werewolves? Guess that explained the sideburns. Wolverine was probably his cousin or something.

"I'm sorry," William said to Claire. "I cannot be involved. But feel free to browse. There are many interesting books in my shop. Books not so dangerous."

Dangerous books. Really? I shrugged, and followed Johan into the third room of the shop. A small hand-lettered sign told me I was in the room of Myths and Legends. The titles ranged from serious research to recent fiction: *Percy Jackson and the Lightning Thief*, *Harry Potter and the Sorcerer's Stone*, *City of Bones, Twilight* ...

I turned to Claire. "So why are these books here?" I asked. "They're not old or rare."

"Because they give us insight into what humans are thinking about the supernatural world. Some humans are gifted—they see beyond the mundane. Not everything in each book is true, but certain elements are."

"So ..." I said nervously, looking over my shoulder. "Do werewolves and vampires really hate each other?"

"Well, maybe not hate," Claire said slowly. "But they're not inclined to go out of their way for each other, as you've just seen."

We continued to browse, moving slowly toward the back of the store. I had just picked up a book on Roman ruins written by my father when the bell chimed softly, signaling that someone had entered the shop. Claire stiffened. I looked toward the front, and saw a tall man in a black coat talking to William. He was dressed like the blond man, but he looked nothing like him. This man had dark hair, dark eyes, and a dark look on his face. Velathri? The cat on the counter arched its back and hissed at the newcomer. The man glanced at the cat, then with a flick of his hand knocked it to the floor.

"How dare you!" William said. "Leave my shop at once!"

I stood frozen as the man leaned toward William, menace in every movement. "Do not cross me, friend," the man said. His voice was low and gravelly, and didn't sound friendly at all. Chills ran up my spine as he spoke. "Now where is it?"

"Where is what?" William asked, standing straight before the dark figure.

"The book. You had it once before, and I know it has found its way back to you."

"Not this time. Even if someone brought it to me, I would refuse it," William said. "I don't want trouble."

The cat was crouched in the corner, ears laid flat and tail twitching. His eyes didn't leave the man.

"I'll take a look around to make sure," the man said. "And if I find it …."

"Fine," William said. "Go ahead."

I had no idea what was going on, but I knew we couldn't let the man see us. I began to edge toward the back room of the store, a messy office with head-high stacks of unshelved books. Maybe we could hide in there. Claire and Johan slipped through the door just ahead of me.

Suddenly, the dark man turned toward the back of the shop. "Who's there?" he asked William.

"Just the cat," William said, shrugging. "He doesn't like you."

I watched the cat in the next room jump from a stack of books to a nearby chair. The stack of books wobbled, then fell over with a soft thump.

"Come on," Claire hissed. "The cat's giving us time to get away."

I tore myself from the scene in front of me, and looked at what Claire was doing. She'd opened a trapdoor hidden under a throw rug, and Johan was already halfway down the stairs. I followed him, and Claire hooked the throw rug to the handle of the trapdoor with a loop that must have been put there for that purpose, and pulled both down over our heads. I looked around. We were in a cellar. I realized I could see because Claire was glowing.

"Claire? You're—"

"Later," she said, leading the way toward the back of the underground room. Behind a bookshelf, there was a door that led to a tunnel. I wanted more of an explanation than that, but considering the possibility of mortal danger, I decided to let it go for now.

"What's that?" Johan said, pointing at the book I was holding. I looked down. I'd completely forgotten about it.

"My dad wrote it. I didn't mean to take it—I had it in my hand when the man came in the store."

"It's okay. William will understand. If it makes you feel better, you can return it or pay him for it later," Claire said. "If we go back right now, we put him in danger as well, not just us. Come on, we've got to get out of here."

"And how are we going to do that?" I asked my glowing friend.

"These tunnels lead to safe houses all over the city," she replied.

"How do you know this?" More secrets. I felt my temper flaring again.

"Garda know all the escape routes of a city where they live. We're quite capable of fighting, but the results are hard to explain to human investigators. And the memories of any humans who happen to witness an altercation must be erased. It causes an incredible amount of work. So we prefer stealth," Claire said. "Now come."

We followed her gentle glow down a maze of tunnels. I could see palmetto bugs, basically huge flying roaches, scuttling ahead of us. I shuddered. I was glad when we finally reached a ladder that led to another trapdoor. I tucked the book into the waistband of my shorts, and climbed up behind Johan. He pushed on the trapdoor, lifting it cautiously.

"No one around," he whispered.

We climbed out, shutting the trapdoor behind us. I stood up and looked around. We were in the storage room of a restaurant. I sniffed. A pizza restaurant. I looked at the boxes stacked on shelves around me. The Mellow Mushroom. Claire cracked the storeroom door, peered out, and waved us through.

We were standing beside the restroom doors. To the right was the kitchen, and to the left was the dining room. It was lunchtime. We could hear the clink of glasses and a hum of conversation from the dining room. A waiter stopped, staring at us.

"Can I help you?" he asked. He was young, probably a college student waiting tables as a summer job. His nametag said Robbie.

"Yes, I think we got lost," Claire said, giving him her brightest smile. "Is there a table free? We'd like to eat."

"Sure. I just cleaned one right here," he said, pointing to a table just inside the dining room, well away from the front windows. Most people would consider it the worst seat in the house, but then most people weren't hiding from vampires who wanted to kill them.

"Perfect," Claire said. "Thank you, Robbie." She led us toward the table, grabbing three menus from the waiter's station as she walked by.

As we settled into the chairs, I asked, "So what are we doing now?"

"We're eating lunch," Claire said. "And then we'll go shopping. We have to look normal, remember?"

"But what about the book?"

"Put it in your purse," she said. "We'll return it another time. We can't go back to the bookstore today. They may be watching it. And besides, we have bigger problems to deal with."

"Come on, Katie," Johan said. "A dangerous vampire in a black coat is chasing us and you're worried about paying for a book?"

Suddenly, I remembered Claire glowing in the tunnels underneath our feet.

"Hey, Claire," I said. "So how are you able to glow?"

"What, you mean shining?" she said, looking surprised. "All Garda can do that."

"You mean my mother can, um, shine?"

"Sure," Claire said.

"And you didn't mention this earlier? Why haven't I seen it before? Do you turn it on and off?"

"You haven't seen it before because I didn't want you to. Yes, I turn it on and off."

We stopped talking as Robbie came to take our order. When he returned with three Cokes and a large pepperoni and mushroom pizza, I realized I was starving. That bowl of Cheerios hadn't lasted very long. Johan and I made small talk, discussing music and books and college choices while we ate. Claire kept her eyes on the front window, joining in our conversation occasionally without looking at us. Soon, the pizza was gone.

"You guys stay here," she said. "I'll go pay, and look around while I'm up front." She was smiling when she came back. "All clear," she said. "Let's head for the Market."

We continued down King Street, stopping to look in the occasional shop window.

"Katie, you need to buy something," Claire said. "We're shopping for your trip to Italy, remember?"

I was in front of Half-Moon Outfitters. A mannequin in the window was wearing a sleeveless black dress made of some kind of wrinkle-free knit fabric. It had a scoop neck and was snug through the bodice, flaring slightly at the hem, which looked like it would hit about six inches above my knees.

"My mom wants me to take a dress, and that one's perfect. It doesn't look little-girly, and it won't wrinkle in my suitcase."

"Let's go in, then," Claire said.

We entered the cool dimness of the store, Johan heading over to the men's section while Claire and I found the dress in my size.

"Go on," she said. "Try it on."

I found an empty dressing room and slid the dress over my head. I loved it. It fit perfectly, and I'd been right about the mature factor. I looked twenty-five, not almost seventeen. Hmm. Except for the ponytail and running shoes. I pulled the elastic out of my hair and fluffed my curls with my fingers. I slipped off my shoes and stepped out into the store barefooted, twirling to show off the dress.

"Oh." Johan sounded like he'd been punched in the stomach. He'd rejoined Claire while I was in the dressing room. Now he was standing there with a blank look on his face.

"I think it looks good," I said.

"It looks great," Claire said. "I'd say it's a definite yes. What do you think, Johan?"

Johan swallowed, and then croaked out, "Sure. It's fine."

Fine? Really? That's all he could say? I looked at him, my eyebrows raised.

"I like it! Buy it," he said, sounding more normal. "I'll wait outside."

I watched him walk toward the door, wondering what was wrong. I shrugged and decided not to let Johan's reaction bother me. What do guys know about dresses, anyway? I changed back into my t-shirt and shorts, pulling my hair back into its habitual ponytail.

I took the dress to the counter, and had to dig around the book to get to my money. I paid, frowning as I tried to fit everything back in the tiny purse. Finally, I put the book into the shopping bag that held the dress. Much better. It made my purse lighter, too, so the strap didn't cut into my shoulder so much.

We exited the store and turned onto Market Street. The crowds of tourists were thickest here.

Restaurants, shops, and of course the Market itself drew both tourists and locals. We maneuvered our way down crowded sidewalks, admiring the nimble fingers of women weaving sea grass into baskets.

We swerved around a kid who'd stopped in the middle of the sidewalk while he tried to catch the drips from a rapidly melting ice cream cone. The narrow one-way streets were clogged with pedestrians, bicyclists, horse-drawn carriages, and of course the few brave (or foolish) souls in cars looking in vain for empty parking spaces.

June is my favorite month in Charleston. School is out, it's not too hot and humid (yet), and the biting insects haven't had time to multiply. I took a deep breath, breathing in the scents around me— waffle cones, the stables the carriage horses lived in, the briny smell of the marsh just a couple of blocks away.

The trees were bright green and the sky was turquoise, washed clean by spring rains. The clouds were so fluffy and white they looked Photoshopped. We stopped at the fudge shop and took the salesgirl up on her offer of a free sample. I sighed. This was how I had planned to spend my summer. All of it, not just this afternoon.

Stop feeling sorry for yourself, I thought. *You're going to Italy, so live with it.*

Someone bumped into me as I licked the last of the fudge off my fingertips.

"Oh, excuse me," said a man dressed in a Hawaiian shirt and khaki shorts. "I apologize."

"No problem," I said, stepping back. The man was short and round. The top of his bald head was turning pink in the Charleston sun, and sweat poured off of him like he'd just run a 10K. His smile didn't quite reach his eyes, which were small and close-set.

I wondered why visitors to Charleston felt it necessary to wear Hawaiian shirts. Hello! We're on the East Coast! We're not anywhere near those Polynesian islands in the Pacific Ocean that make up the state of Hawaii, which was, by the way, the last state to join the Union. Okay, so we're proud of our history in Charleston. But I get tired of people thinking a beach is a beach is a beach.

As I finished my little internal rant, Hawaiian shirt guy turned and disappeared into the crowd.

"Let's buy some fudge," I said to Claire and Johan. "My mom makes great dinners, but we can bring dessert."

I reached for my purse, but it wasn't there. Hawaiian shirt guy—he must have cut the strap and taken it!

"Claire! Johan! That guy took my purse!'

They both looked at me like I was nuts.

"What guy?" Claire said.

"The one who bumped into me! The bald guy wearing the Hawaiian shirt!"

"Almost every guy here is wearing a Hawaiian shirt," Johan said.

"Wait. Your purse is gone?" Claire said, turning even paler than she was normally. "What was in it?"

"Just a hairbrush, lip gloss, and a change purse with some cash. I left my real wallet at the house."

"Nothing with your name and address on it?"

"No, I already packed my wallet for Italy, so I just brought cash with me."

"Good, because if someone took your purse, I'm afraid they may have been looking for information about who you are or where you live."

"At least I still have William's book," I said. "I put it in the bag with my dress. I would feel so bad if it got stolen before I could return it! But my money is gone. And I liked that purse!"

Claire smiled. "I'll buy the fudge. Money is replaceable, and so are purses. But you aren't."

"What did the guy look like?" Johan asked. "I didn't see anyone who looked suspicious."

"He looked like a tourist—you know, Hawaiian shirt, khaki shorts, and old man shoes. He was sunburnt and sweating—I don't think he's used to our weather."

"So not from here … but probably not a real tourist," Claire said. "Tourists don't steal teenage girls' purses. They're too busy making sure their own pockets don't get picked."

"Yeah. And his outfit was almost too perfect—like he was trying to look like a tourist," I said thoughtfully. "All he was missing was a straw hat."

"We need to head back to your house and let the others know what's happened," Claire said. "I didn't think we were being followed, but between that guy in William's shop and the 'tourist' stealing your purse, I'm starting to get a little nervous."

8

We took Anson Street back, avoiding the more crowded areas so Claire could watch for anyone who might be following us. City noises receded into the distance as the neighborhood became more residential. The streets were empty since it wasn't quite time for people to begin coming home from work. Claire stopped two houses from mine, stepping behind a six-foot tall hedge of camellia bushes and motioning for us to follow.

"Ouch," I whispered as Johan stepped on my foot.

"Sorry," he whispered back.

"*Shh*!" Claire hissed.

I peered over her shoulder, trying to see what she was staring at. The guy who had followed us into the bookstore was walking back and forth in front of my house, his long dark coat flapping behind him each time he turned.

"He's not even trying to hide," Claire said softly. "I wonder what that means."

"My mom!" I said. "We've got to get in there!"

"Wait, Katie," Claire said, blocking me with her arm. "She's safe as long as she's inside. Just hold on and let me think."

I grabbed Johan's arm for balance as I stood on tiptoe, trying to get a good look at the stranger. Just then, Johan's parents turned the corner onto Elizabeth Street from the other end. I heard Johan suck in a breath. He took a step toward the street, but I was holding on to his arm so tightly he had to stop. Claire motioned for us to stay where we were. She began to drift closer to the stranger, who had turned to watch Edward and Juliana approach. They didn't hesitate as they walked toward him.

"Where is it?" the man hissed at them as they neared.

"Where is what?" Edward asked. He and Juliana stood calmly, arms held loosely at their sides. I noticed they were dressed oddly, in dark, close-fitting pants and shirts. I realized the stranger was wearing the same outfit under his long coat. What was with the black outfit? Some kind of vampire uniform?

Suddenly, a blonde woman who glowed so brightly I had to look away stepped between the stranger and Johan's parents.

"Leave this place," she said. "We do not have what you seek."

The dark man hissed, then turned on his heel and disappeared. I stared. He was just gone. How had he done that? And where was Claire? I'd been so focused on the stranger and Johan's parents I'd lost sight of her. Wait. Claire was standing where the bright woman had been a second ago. *Claire* was the glowing woman.

"You can let go any time now," Johan said to me. I realized I had his arm in a death grip.

"Oh, sorry," I said. He rubbed where my hands had been.

"You're stronger than you think, you know," he said, grinning.

"Did you see that?" I asked. "Did you see Claire?"

"Yeah, that's her real form," Johan said, shrugging. "I've seen it before."

"Wait. When?" I demanded.

"When she comes over to talk to my parents, she comes in her adult form. It took me a few years to figure it out, but I did," Johan said.

"And you never told me."

"Would you have believed me?" he asked.

He had a point. I would have thought he was either hallucinating or teasing me. Now, however, I'd seen it myself. We stepped out from behind the camellia bushes and walked toward Johan's parents and Claire, who was back in teenage girl form.

"What just happened?" I asked.

"The Velathri apparently think we have the book," Edward said gravely. "It's definitely in Charleston. There's unusual movement in the supernatural world here. But we weren't able to get a lock on it."

"Let's go in before Sergio returns with reinforcements," Claire said.

Juliana nodded. "We should save our strength," she said. "Fighting now will just deplete us."

"Sergio? Who's that?" I demanded.

"An old friend," Edward said.

"Uh, weren't you pretty rude to your friend?"

"Sometimes a friend, and sometimes an enemy," Claire said. "I didn't want to take any chances."

I turned that over in my mind as we straggled in to the kitchen. My mom, Adam and Ariel were already there.

"What did you buy?" my mom asked, looking at the Half-Moon Outfitters bag in my hand.

"A dress for the trip," I answered, pulling the dress out. "It's perfect—comfortable, won't wrinkle, and it looks grown-up."

"Maybe a little too grown-up," my mom said, examining it.

"Oh, Libby, it is time," Ariel said. "You cannot keep her a child forever. I think it is lovely," she added, turning to me. "But what else is in the bag?"

"Oh, a book my dad wrote," I said, pulling it out and putting it on the table in front of me.

Adam stared. "Where did you get that?"

"At an old bookstore. I'll go back and pay for it, I promise," I said.

"Wait, you didn't pay for it?" my mom said, raising her eyebrows at me.

"Well, we were being chased by some guy who looked like a Velathri ..." my voice trailed off as her face paled.

"Let me tell the story," Claire said, getting up and handing my mom a glass of ice water. "We saw William," she said. The others nodded. Apparently everyone knew who he was. "He owns a bookstore that Johan knew about."

"Yeah, but I didn't know the old guy was a werewolf," Johan said. "I just thought maybe whoever stole the book might have tried to sell it there."

"Not a bad theory," Adam said.

"But while we were there, Sergio came in the store and asked about the book Johan lost," Claire said. "We were in the back, so I led Katie and Johan out through the tunnels, and he never saw us."

"And he was out front just now," Juliana said. "Edward and I were prepared to fight, but Claire appeared in her light form, and he left."

"I'm not happy they've found this house," Adam said. "We'll have to rethink our strategy."

"So tell me about this book," my mom said, pointing at the volume I'd placed on the kitchen table.

"I was holding it when that guy came in the bookstore. I didn't realize I had it in my hand when we ran," I said. "It's one of Dad's."

Mom looked closer. "Your father never wrote a book called *Roman Ruins*," she said. "Let me see it."

I peered over her shoulder as she opened the small leather volume. Inside was a second cover, green leather, with the words *Rulers of Ireland* embossed in gold. There was silence in the room.

"That's the book!" Johan exclaimed. "That's it! Katie, how did you find it?"

"I … I don't know," I stuttered. "I just picked it up."

"Hmm," Ariel said. "It must have a spell on it. When enemies get close, it reappears in another place. I have heard of such spells. That is very powerful magic. I wonder how your father managed it."

"So why was I able to carry it out of the bookstore?" I asked.

"Someone or something obviously wanted you to find it. That may be part of the spell. If we are to keep it in our possession, we must keep it safe. Otherwise, it will disappear again," Ariel said.

"Oh, and a tourist stole my purse, too," I said, suddenly remembering the guy in the Hawaiian shirt.

Everyone stared at me again. I was really getting tired of this.

"Claire?" Adam said, a question in his voice.

"I was getting to that part," Claire said. "We were in the Market, eating fudge."

"You went to the Market?" Adam said, raising his eyebrows.

Claire shrugged. "We were doing what normal teenagers do when they're out of school. And while we were there, a man dressed like a tourist bumped into Katie and cut the strap on her purse. We decided he probably wasn't a real tourist. But there was nothing to identify her in the purse—just some money."

"That decides it. We cannot stay here in Charleston. We must leave for Italy immediately," Adam said.

"But what about graduation? Claire and I are junior marshals!" I protested.

"We are talking about not only your life, but also the lives of millions of supernatural beings and humans, too, if a war breaks out over these books," Edward said. "We must get this book to Montepulciano, and reunite it with its companion volume."

Claire cleared her throat. "I have the other book," she said. "I had no idea Tony would hide this one in Charleston."

There was silence as her news sank in.

"Where is it?" Adam said, looking angry. "It is far too dangerous to have them this close to each other outside Montepulciano."

Supernatural beings who protect others also keep secrets from each other. Interesting.

"Under dirty clothes in the back of my closet."

"What?"

"Where better to hide something valuable than in a teenager's bedroom?" she shrugged. "I make sure to keep it a mess."

"Well, that explains a lot," Ariel said. "I was beginning to worry you really thought you were an American teenager."

"This is bad," Adam said. "We have to travel separately, each group with one of the books. The Velathri getting one would be bad, but the Velathri getting both would be disaster. We must leave as soon as we can—tomorrow morning if possible."

Well, this just sucked. I hadn't been thrilled about the summer in Italy to begin with, but adding in evil vampires who wanted to kill me just made it so much better. And missing graduation was the last straw.

"Mom!" I said. "Graduation! You promised!"

I knew I was acting like a whiny brat, but I couldn't help myself. I had never asked to be some kind of vampire hero. I'd been kept in the dark about who I really was, and now everyone was acting like I should feel honored to have my entire life, everything I'd ever believed about myself and my family, ripped to shreds.

"I know, honey," she said gently. "But this is more important. I'll call Principal Puckett and let him know you and Claire won't be there."

I felt tears prick the back of my eyelids. I so did not want to cry in front of these people. I turned and ran up the stairs, slamming my door and throwing myself on my bed. I let the tears come, crying over graduation, but also crying over my lost future, letting go of the fantasy that I was a normal human girl who would grow up to do normal human things.

Eventually, I sat up and wiped my eyes with the back of my hand. I went in the bathroom and splashed my face with cold water. My eyes and nose were red, my face swollen from crying. Great, I looked like a clown. Not that it mattered. I'm sure the Velathri wouldn't care what I looked like when they came to kill me.

Claire knocked softly, then opened the door and came in, closing the door behind her.

"Are you okay?" she said. "I know this is hard. It wasn't supposed to be this way. You were supposed to be told about your heritage by your parents; you were supposed to go to classes."

"Classes? What kind of classes? There are classes on how to be a vampire?"

"History classes. Classes where you'd learn all the stuff that I've tried to tell you yesterday and today. There's a lot more you need to know, but it can wait. Right now, you need to come downstairs and eat. We'll tell you the plan for tomorrow, and then we all need to get some sleep."

I looked at Claire. "First, there are some things I need to know."

Claire looked at the serious expression on my face.

"Okay," she said, sitting down. "Ask me."

"You've been my friend—my best friend—since fourth grade," I said. "And now I find out you're, you're …" my voice trailed off.

"Something else?" Claire prompted.

"Yes. Something else. Maybe not my friend at all," I said. "What's real and what's not? I'm upset not just because I might become a vampire, although I find that incredibly gross, but it seems that none of the people in my life are who I thought they were, either."

"Katie, I know this is hard," Claire began.

"You think?" I snorted, and then realized that was a really bad idea right after a crying jag. I stood up and went into the bathroom to blow my nose.

"Listen," Claire said. "I didn't decide to keep you in the dark. That was your parents."

"Yes, but that wasn't my question," I said, turning to stand in the door of the bathroom. "How much of our friendship is real, and how much was just you playing a part?"

"Katie, I love you like a daughter," Claire said.

I snorted again. "That's not exactly the same as a best friend," I said.

"No, it's not," Claire said. "And I'm sorry you feel betrayed. But this deception was necessary for me to be close to you on a daily basis. It's my assignment to keep you safe."

I had my answer. We weren't and had never been best friends. I was her assignment. She loved me like a daughter. Maybe she should just go ahead and drop the teen look, too. I took a deep breath, blew my nose again, and followed Claire to the kitchen.

CHAPTER NINE

9

My mom had made sandwiches. There wasn't time for much else. As I ate, Adam outlined the plan for tomorrow. We would travel in three groups. Mom, Claire, and I would fly out first, carrying the book I'd found today. Claire reasoned that if the spell protecting the book had let me find it, then the book would probably stay with me instead of disappearing again.

Adam and Ariel would go back to their house, get the book Claire had hidden in her closet, and travel together to Italy. Edward and Juliana would leave the house first, then circle back to make sure none of us were followed as we left for the airport. They would fly out with Johan tomorrow. Our tickets had been purchased online, and our passports were all up to date. Good thing I'd already packed.

I finished my sandwich and started loading the dishwasher. That way, I could keep my back turned on everyone. Johan came over, carrying plates from the table. He began helping me without speaking. As we worked side by side, I finally relaxed. At least one person in my world was who I had always thought he was. His presence comforted me more than any words could have.

"Our success depends on speed and surprise," Adam said. "We must be quick in the morning. No hesitation. Now off to bed, everyone."

Apparently, everyone was staying at my house. Johan was on the couch in the den. Adam and Ariel were in the guest room. Claire was with me again. Edward and Juliana took guard duty. I wondered when they planned to sleep? Wait. They were vampires—no need to sleep. This would take some getting used to. Claire and I went upstairs, and only a few tears leaked out before I fell asleep. The next thing I knew, my mom was shaking me awake. It was still dark outside. Claire's bed was neatly made, and her suitcase was gone.

"Katie, wake up. We need to go," Mom whispered.

I nodded, threw back the covers and stumbled to the bathroom. I threw on a t-shirt, jeans, and my running shoes. I pulled my hair into a pony tail and tossed my make-up case into my big rolling suitcase. I picked up my new espadrilles, shrugged, and added them. I tied the arms of a hooded sweatshirt around my waist in case I got cold on the plane. My phone, my wallet, and my passport were already in my backpack. I grabbed my suitcase and headed downstairs. As I entered the kitchen, I could smell bacon, eggs, and grits. My mom was putting steaming platters of food on the table.

"Mom," I said. "Cereal would have been fine."

"It's going to be a long day," she replied. "Eat while you can."

Claire and Johan were at the table, already eating. Edward and Juliana were unloading the dishwasher. I sat and served my plate.

We all froze at a knock on the front door. Adam stood up. He and Juliana headed for the back door while my mom headed for the front. Once outside, Adam and Juliana split up—one going left and the other going right.

My mom waited at the front door until Adam yelled, "Okay, Libby, open the door!"

Mom opened the door to find Adam and Juliana holding up the blond guy in the black coat that I had seen on the last day of school.

"Alex!" my mom cried, pushing Juliana out of the way to take his left arm and help him in to the house.

What? She knew this guy? And she also acted like she really cared that he was hurt. Okay. That was weird. Adam and Mom gently helped the guy onto our couch. He was even paler than he'd been two days ago when I'd seen him on the way to school. Blood oozed from two small puncture marks on his neck.

"He bit me," the guy rasped. "Sergio. He bit me."

"He didn't drain you," Adam said. "He wants to warn you, not kill you. Here."

As I watched in amazement, Adam held out his wrist. The guy bit into the artery and began drinking. After a minute, he stopped and my mom took Adam's place. After another minute, he stopped and leaned back, his eyes closed. Claire sat with him, her face pale, holding the guy's head in her lap.

"Mom! What's going on here," I hissed as she came out of the parlor into the hallway.

"Come to the kitchen," she whispered. "I'll explain."

"Don't you need a bandage?" I asked.

She held up her wrist, and I realized that the wound had already healed.

"Okay," I said as we reached the kitchen. "Answers, mom. I need answers. I thought that guy was a Garda."

"He is."

"But he was drinking your blood."

"He is also a vampire. He is the only other half-fairy, half-vampire that we know of," she answered.

"Only other ... besides me, you mean," I said.

"Yes. He's my half-brother, and your uncle. The blood from a vampire and a fairy will heal him. That's why Adam and I both gave him our blood."

Just then, my newfound uncle walked into the kitchen. Up close, I could see he looked a lot like my mother. He had a kind face, and twinkling blue eyes.

"Hello, Katie," he said, holding out his hand. "I'm your Uncle Alex."

I couldn't think of anything to say, so I just took his hand and shook it.

"I understand you have some questions," he said.

I did know what to say to this.

"Yes. And the first one is why didn't anyone tell me about this sooner?"

"Your parents thought it would help keep you safe if you didn't know," my newfound uncle said. "But the time of your adulthood is nearing, and you need to know what is coming."

"Why are you here now?"

"Because I, like you, am half-fairy and half-vampire. What happens to us is not like what happens to half-human/half-vampires. They get to choose. And many of them choose to remain human.

We have no choice. We receive parts of both beings, becoming something entirely different."

"Will I," I swallowed. "I know this is silly, but will my hair turn blonde? Are my eyes going to turn blue?"

Finding out I wasn't just an ordinary teenage girl looking forward to college was hard enough. I didn't know if I could take a complete makeover.

Alex and my mother both laughed. "No," he answered. "You'll still look like you. I'm fair because my father and mother were both fair. You look like your father, and you always will."

Well, that was a relief.

"So what about drinking blood?"

"You'll be able to drink blood for sustenance and for healing," Alex said. "But it's not necessary to your survival, as it is for full vampires."

"Will I live forever?"

"We don't know that yet, now do we?" Alex said. "So far, so good, though. I'm two hundred years old, and I show no signs of aging. You are fast, you are strong, and you heal quickly. You may manifest other gifts later, after your seventeenth birthday."

Two hundred years old. Maybe that explained his strange word choices. Manifest? Seriously? Just then, Adam came in, looking tense.

"Libby, you and the girls have to leave now if you're going to make it to the airport on time," he said. "I've called a cab and it should be here in five minutes."

My mom nodded. "Katie, Claire, get your suitcases. We'll continue this conversation in Italy." She gave Alex a hug. "Be careful," she whispered, kissing him on the cheek.

He looked at her fondly. "I always am, little sister," he said, hugging her back.

Claire and I took our suitcases and stood by the front door. My new uncle stood beside Claire, his arm around her shoulder. So they knew each other, too. Fairly well, it looked like to me. Adam went out to make sure that Sergio, our Velathri friend, wasn't still hanging around. Juliana checked the backyard, and Johan joined us awkwardly in the hall. I looked at him.

"This isn't what I thought summer vacation would be like," I said.

"Me, neither," he said. "But at least I get to go with you now."

As the taxi pulled up, Adam waved all clear to us. My mom went first, then Claire. Uncle Alex followed, helping the cab driver load the luggage in the trunk. As I took the handle of my suitcase, preparing to step off the porch, Johan stepped closer and wrapped his arms around me in a hug. I wrapped my arms around his waist and leaned my head on his chest, realizing he was tall enough for his chin to rest on the top of my head. Wow. When had that happened?

"Katie, come on!" Claire hissed, leaning out of the door of the cab. "This is dangerous!"

As I stood there, unwilling to let go, Johan said, "Katie, it'll be okay. I'll be there soon."

I turned and ran down the steps, glad that if I had to go to Italy, at least Johan was coming, too. I folded myself into the back seat beside Claire.

"We're going to the airport," my mom told the driver. "International terminal."

We were silent as the taxi maneuvered through mostly empty streets. I could see a sliver of light edging over the horizon, turning the sky pink. I concentrated on breathing slowly and getting my emotions under control. I hadn't wanted to go to Italy to begin with, and I realized I was steaming mad at both my mom and Claire. They may have thought they were keeping me safe by not telling me the truth of my heritage, but the hurt and betrayal I felt was going to take a while to heal.

As we pulled up to the International Terminal of the Charleston airport, I realized that until now, to me, Claire had been my best friend. I'd shared everything with her. But she wasn't really a seventeen-year-old girl. And she wasn't just a protector. She was the perfect chaperone.

I stared at the back of my mom's head. *Super sneaky, there, Mom*, I thought, narrowing my eyes. I thought through conversations I'd had with Claire about my parents' divorce—how I'd told her how angry and hurt I was. How I'd complained about going to Italy this summer. Okay, now that made me really angry. Having a Garda as a best friend was turning out to be bad in lots of different ways. A super powerful nanny disguised as someone my own age was more like it. She had said she loved me like a daughter. Yeah, I was beginning to understand what that meant.

My mom paid the taxi driver, and we lined up at the Lufthansa counter. Flying the German airline to Italy would be unexpected, and we hoped that would throw off anyone who might be watching our movements. Claire looked around, on alert as my mom checked us in. All of our luggage could be carried on—nothing to check, nothing to slow us down at the airport in Rome.

My mom walked us toward the metal detectors at double time. It was so early there were only a few people in the airport. A young couple with a baby was going through security ahead of us. The guard was going over the stroller and diaper bag as though the infant were hiding grenades between his diapers and wipes. An elderly couple came to stand in line behind us. Claire gave them a sharp look, and then went back to scanning the area around us.

We took off our shoes and put them in the gray bins along with our cell phones, keys, and quart zip-lock bags of liquids and gels. We walked through the scanners and collected our belongings. As I straightened up after tying my sneakers, I realized Claire and my mom had moved ahead of me. I grabbed my backpack and suitcase and hurried after them.

The only warning I had was a flash of movement on my left, then everything went black. I couldn't see. I couldn't breathe. I realized something had been put over my head. I let go of my suitcase to pull at whatever it was, and I heard a clatter as my suitcase fell over. Suddenly, the hands holding me down released me. I pulled a cloth sack off of my head, and saw Claire had pinned my attacker. He groaned as she twisted his arms.

"Who sent you?" she hissed.

"It's not worth my life to tell you," the man said, moaning as Claire twisted his arms again.

"Katie, get your bag and go. I'll follow you."

Stunned, I did what she said. My mother was waiting at the entrance to the jetway. I turned, watching as three security guards surged toward Claire and the man, their guns pulled.

"I'll handle it. Go," my mom said, shoving me onto the jetway.

I entered, rubbing my neck where the man had clutched the sack closed after pulling it over my head. I smiled at the stewardess, trying to look like I hadn't almost been abducted on my way to her plane.

She looked at my ticket, and said brightly, "About halfway down on the left. If you need help putting your suitcase in the overhead bin, let me know!"

I stashed my suitcase and sat down in the window seat, waiting for my mom and Claire to join me. The plane gradually filled. Passengers trickled in, found spots for their suitcases, settled in to their seats, held whispered conversations, pulled out books, sent last-minute text messages. But the two seats beside me remained empty. Where were my mom and Claire? They were supposed to be right behind me.

I saw the two stewardesses holding a whispered conversation at the front of the cabin. Then the one who had welcomed me onto the plane closed the door and locked it. I tried to stand, and then realized my seat belt was fastened.

"Wait," I said, waving my hands to get their attention. The other stewardess came toward me.

"There are two passengers who aren't on board," I said. "My mom and my friend."

"I'm sorry," she said. "We paged the airport, and we've waited ten minutes past the time we should have left the gate. We have to leave now."

"Then let me off!" I said, struggling to unhook my seatbelt.

"We can't. It's too late ," she said. "I'm sorry. They'll have to catch the next flight."

I felt a jerk as the plane began to back away from the terminal.

"No!" I said. "I can't go to Italy without them!"

10

J ust wait in the Rome airport by baggage claim," the stewardess, whose name was Heather, said. "The next flight is only thirty minutes behind this one. I'll tell you what. I'll radio back and make sure they're on it. What're their names?"

"Elizabeth LeGare and Claire Corbett," I told her, still stunned by the fact I was on the plane alone. I would land in Rome alone. And my mom and Claire might or might not arrive thirty minutes later.

Heather smiled brightly and nodded, turning toward the cockpit. I took a deep breath and tried to think. A guy had tried to kidnap me. Claire had stopped him, and my mom had gone to help her. That was two against one. They would be all right, especially since Claire had the guy on the ground the last time I'd seen them. They'd been delayed because they'd been questioning him, trying to find out what he knew. And security—they had to deal with the human security guards I'd seen running toward them.

That was it. I took a deep breath. There was nothing to be afraid of, I told myself sternly. When I landed in Rome, I would go to baggage claim and wait there for them. But none of us had any baggage to claim. We all had carry-ons. So why would they come to baggage claim to look for me? I shot a look at Heather. She didn't look dangerous. Maybe I was being paranoid. But I wasn't taking any drinks from her, and I wasn't going to baggage claim when I got to Rome.

Once we were in the air and I could turn my cell phone back on, I sent Claire and my mom text messages. I didn't know exactly when they'd get them, but at least I'd done something.

Settling in my seat, I thought about pulling out the *Rulers of Ireland* book and trying to see what made it important enough to kill over, but then I figured if Heather was a spy for the Velathri, there was no need letting her know I had what they wanted. I tried to watch the in-flight movie, but I must have been more tired than I realized. I woke up as Heather and Emma, the other stewardess, started through the cabin offering warm washcloths. I accepted gratefully, scrubbing at the hours of grit coating my face.

I had slept through the airline breakfast, and was starving. The lunch they served was half a sandwich, some chips, and three apple slices. That was it. Seriously. We'd been in the air for nearly eleven hours, and that's what they fed us. It's a good thing I had my debit card. When I hit the Rome airport, the first thing I was looking for was food.

"Ladies and gentlemen, we will be landing in Rome in about thirty minutes," the captain informed us. "It is 9 p.m. local time. The temperature is 81 degrees Fahrenheit, 27 degrees Celsius. The skies are clear."

He repeated the information in German, French, and Italian. It sounded lovely. Except I didn't know where Claire and my mother were. The next time Heather came my way, I flagged her down.

"Were you able to find out if my mom is on the next flight?" I asked.

"I put in the call, but I didn't get an answer right away," she said. "Let me finish what I'm doing, and I'll check again."

As we would be landing in twenty-five minutes or less, I didn't put much faith in Heather's promise. I steeled myself. I was going to be alone in the Rome airport. I needed a plan. First, I needed to eat. I had no way to tell if Heather was lying, or if she really hadn't been able to find out. So it made sense to go to a restaurant in the airport, eat, and wait to see if my mom and Claire showed up. If they didn't, then I would need a Plan B.

So Plan B: I would need a place to stay in Rome. I had no idea where my mom had made reservations. Besides, if people (or Velathri or werewolves or possibly something even worse—I didn't want to think about that) were following me, they'd probably be watching the hotel where we were supposed to go. I had my debit card, and a credit card my mom had given me for emergencies. I could charge a night or two at a hotel. Just not an expensive one.

I decided a small bed and breakfast would work just fine. I needed to get to my dad, but trying to make travel plans and watch out for evil vampires while jet-lagged would be nearly impossible. Food, then sleep, I decided. When I woke up, I would figure out how to get to Montepulciano.

I heard the whine of the landing gear opening. I heard the engines ratchet up as they slowed our descent into Rome. I felt the thunk as we touched down, and held my breath as the pilot braked the huge aircraft, slowing us to a crawl and turning us toward the airport. This was it. I was on my own. And I was carrying a book that I needed to guard with my life. Not to mention guarding my life. And all I'd really wanted out of my summer vacation was a tan and a pedicure.

I pulled my suitcase out of the overhead bin and joined the line of people exiting the plane. Heather was waiting at the doorway.

"I hope you had a nice flight," she said cheerily. "Do you need directions to baggage claim?"

"Why yes," I said, even though I had no intention of going anywhere near baggage claim. "Can you help me?"

"Go to your left, and then follow the signs. You'll go down an escalator and then just look for your flight number on the sign over the belts," Heather said.

"Thanks!" I replied, smiling like she was my new best friend. "You've been so helpful!"

I never, ever wanted to see her insincere smile again. But my mother had brought me up to be polite. Plus, it was probably a good thing if she thought I was an idiot—maybe she wouldn't check to see if I actually went to baggage claim. Because it certainly felt like she was herding me that way. Obediently, I turned left when I reached the terminal. Oh. I had to go through customs first. Crap. But whatever.

There were lots of people around, because it was tourist season in Rome. The airport was bustling, not deserted like the Charleston airport had been early this morning. I tried to convince myself that this made me safer. At least I could blend in and hide behind students on summer trips to Rome. That was definitely a plus. I joined a group of kids from Boston who were in Rome to study architecture. I listened to them chatter about Ionic and Doric and Corinthian arches while I scanned the area for men in long dark coats. I even sniffed the air like Claire had done. I mean, technically, I was half-Garda. Shouldn't it work for me, too? Maybe later I could try to glow. Right. I snorted.

Get real, Katie, I told myself sternly.

What had Claire been sniffing for? I didn't smell anything out of the ordinary. Just students who'd been on a plane since five that morning (a few showers were in order), the industrial cleaners the airport custodians used, and something dark and musty.

Wait. What was *that* smell? I pretended to read a poster listing what was and was not allowed through Customs while trying to pinpoint the odor. How could something smell dark? I couldn't explain it. That's just the feeling I got when it hit my nose—darkness.

As my group of chattering students moved slowly through the chute toward the passport check points, I spotted the odor's source. A man in a black coat—which didn't look so out of place here—was standing half-hidden behind a column. It wasn't Sergio, but at first glance the man looked enough like him to be his brother—beefy, dark haired and dark eyed. I examined him more closely. He was dressed the same, but he was scruffier than the man who had tailed us in Charleston. His hair was long and unkempt, and his long black coat looked like he had slept in it. So hygiene wasn't his top priority. I shrugged. My job was to make sure he didn't spot me, not worry about his bathing habits.

My group was being herded through customs, and I was swept along with them. The customs guy barely glanced at my passport, just stamped it, handed it back and nodded me through. The students I was tagging along with stopped under an information board while they waited on the rest of their group. I checked to see where the next plane from Charleston was arriving. Five gates down, and it was on time. I looked around. There was a little restaurant across from customs.

As the students headed for baggage claim, I peeled off and went through the line, choosing a sandwich, chips, and water. I paid and sat at a table in the rear of the restaurant, my back against the wall. I watched the big guy watching the gate I'd exited. Once he was sure no one else was getting off the plane, he moved closer to the gate I was watching. I went from hoping my mom and Claire were on the plane to hoping they weren't.

I sent a text warning them about our welcoming committee, just in case they were on board. Crap, my cell phone was dying. I needed to charge it. I realized my best chance to leave the airport without being spotted was now, while the guy was waiting for the next plane.

I finished my food, put my backpack on, grabbed my suitcase, and headed for an information kiosk. I found one out of sight of scruffy black-coat guy, and grabbed a subway map and a flyer on hotels and motels. I took the next tunnel downstairs. In *Twilight*, Alice might have been able to hotwire a cool yellow sports car and drive it at top speeds through the winding Italian countryside, but me? I would have to take a train.

The tunnel forked in front of me. Express or local? The express train was faster, but more expensive. And maybe more predictable? I took the tunnel toward the local trains. At the touch-screen kiosk, I bought a ticket that would take me to the end of the line. As I waited on the platform, I scanned the people around me. I took a few deep breaths. If I couldn't detect the dark, musty scent, maybe that meant I wasn't being followed. All I smelled were common subway odors—garbage, urine, unwashed bodies, and that weird oil and electricity smell that subways have, no matter what city or country you're in. I heard the roar of the approaching train and the squeal of brakes as the cars came to a stop in front of me. I entered a car in the middle of the train, finding a seat in the corner.

As the doors closed and the train pulled off, I relaxed and pulled the hotel and motel flyer from my backpack. I needed something small, on the north side of Rome. Why had my mom had us fly in to Rome? I was so far from Florence. It would take me all day to get there tomorrow, and then I still had to get to Montepulciano. I was familiar with the rail routes from Florence to Montepulciano after all the summers we'd spent there. But I'd never been to Rome before, and traveling on my own was confusing, even if I could speak basic Italian.

I looked up to see an old woman dressed all in black staring at me.

"What are you looking for, dear?" she asked in Italian.

"A place to stay," I replied in Italian. "A safe place."

"Yes, a young girl on her own needs to be careful," she answered. "I rent rooms. You can stay with me."

I studied her face. She laughed.

"Oh, I am quite harmless, dear one. You will be very safe with Nonna Maria."

I didn't have a lot of choices. The sun had set, and wandering the streets of Rome after dark looking for a room was not an appealing option. I made a decision.

"Okay. It's a deal."

Worst case, I was pretty sure I could outrun her. Being a track star did have its benefits.

We rode the train to the last stop, then got off and walked through winding, narrow streets to a residential neighborhood about five blocks from the train station. Nonna Maria's house was tall and narrow, like our house in Charleston. But instead of wood siding, it was white-washed stucco, with geraniums blooming a riotous red from the window boxes that hung under every window. Wooden shutters painted green completed the picture. A small sign over the front door read, *Si Affitano Camere*. Rooms for Rent.

Okay, so the old lady hadn't been lying. She really did rent rooms.

"Breakfast comes with the room. Have you eaten dinner?"

"I had a sandwich at the airport," I said.

"That's not enough to keep you alive," Nonna Maria said. "Come. Cooking for two is no more trouble than cooking for one."

She led me to the kitchen at the back of the house. A large stone fireplace, big enough for me to walk into, was the focal point. No fire burned in it right now, but it was obviously still in use.

"Sit," she commanded. I sat at the wide plank table and looked around the room while Nonna Maria busied herself at the gas stove. The wooden floor gleamed and white lace curtains fluttered in the breeze blowing through the open window. It felt incredibly homey.

"Breakfast for dinner," she said as she put a plate filled with a sausage omelette, pan-fried potatoes, and Italian bread in front of me. She pulled a platter of sliced tomatoes from the refrigerator and poured me a glass of milk before sitting down across from me.

I ate in silence for a few minutes, looking up only when she asked, "Why is a young girl like you traveling alone in Italy?"

"My mom missed the plane," I said. "I don't know when she'll get here, so I decided to go on to where my dad is."

"Why didn't your father meet your plane?" she asked.

"He doesn't know we're here. We were supposed to arrive next week, but decided to leave early."

"You need to let him know. If your mother has called him, then he will be worried."

Nonna Maria took my plate to the sink and washed it, putting it on a drying rack. There was no dishwasher. She disappeared into the next room and returned with a cordless phone. So some technology was available, at least.

"Here," she said. "Call him."

Why hadn't I thought of this? Now that she said it, it made perfect sense. I dialed my dad's cell number. He answered on the second ring.

"Pronto?"

"Dad, it's me, Katie," I said in English, eyeing Nonna Maria. She was busy cleaning up, so I figured she couldn't understand.

"Katie! Where are you?" he answered.

"I'm in Rome. At a bed and breakfast."

"Are you safe?" he interrupted me.

"I think I am. It's a small place on the northern side of Rome. Someone named Nonna Maria owns it."

"Let me talk to her," Dad said.

I handed the phone to Nonna Maria. She nodded a couple of times, answering in Italian spoken so quickly I only caught a few words, then handed the phone back to me.

"Where are Mom and Claire? Have you heard from them? Why didn't they get on the plane?"

I would have kept asking questions, but Dad stopped me.

"Whoa," he said. "One question at a time. Your mom and Claire are fine. They missed the plane because of the guy who tried to grab you. They took him to the Garda headquarters in Charleston, and he's being questioned there. They'll fly in tomorrow, but don't wait for them. Catch the morning train to Florence, and I'll meet you there. I'll drive you to Montepulciano."

"Is it safe to take the Express?"

"Yes, it should be. But keep your eyes open. You're safe where you are tonight, so sleep well."

"But, Dad, I have so many questions."

"I'll try to answer them tomorrow," he said. "But now, you need to rest. Ciao, Mia Bella," he said, using his childhood nickname for me.

"Ciao, Papa," I replied, hanging up the phone.

I was glad to know Mom and Claire were safe, but it had been an extremely unsatisfactory conversation.

"So, was I right?" Nonna Maria asked in Italian.

"Yes, he was worried. And he'll meet me at the train station in Florence tomorrow," I answered.

"Good. I knew a lovely girl like you must have family around to take care of her. Now, let me show you to your room."

Apparently, there were no other guests. Nonna Maria took me upstairs and opened the door to a large room with a huge bed covered with the thickest down coverlet I'd ever seen. Four down pillows were propped against the headboard, and the bathroom off the bedroom was floored in marble. It was beautiful, and all I could do to keep my eyes open long enough to brush my teeth and fall into the bed.

"Good night, Mia Bella," Nonna Maria said softly as she left, closing the door behind her. I was so tired I barely noticed she'd used my dad's pet name for me.

The next morning, Nonna Maria made two sandwiches—fried egg, provolone cheese, and prosciutto on toasted Italian bread. One she put on a plate on the table, and the other she wrapped up and put in my backpack.

"Eat up," she said. "We must leave in twenty minutes to get to the train station on time."

Wow. The sandwich was wonderful. That beat Cheerios every time. I could have eaten both sandwiches right then. But instead, I ran upstairs and grabbed my suitcase. As I closed the door to the room behind me, I looked up. The familiar three circles of the triskelion were carved into the wooden lintel above the door. I sucked in my breath. This was a safe house. I hadn't ended up here by chance. I slowly walked down the stairs, trying to figure out who Nonna Maria really was. At least now I knew there were helpful creatures as well as murderous vampires watching me.

"Hurry," Nonna Maria said, looking pointedly at the clock. "We must go now."

I could see more of the neighborhood this time as we retraced our steps to the train station. The early morning sun lit up the front of the bakery, which was doing brisk business. The butcher was just unlocking his door, and the bistro was quiet. A few people sat at sidewalk tables outside a coffee shop, and the bells of the cathedral chimed seven times.

What a beautiful day. I wanted to stay and explore Rome. I wanted to be a normal girl on a normal trip. But that wasn't going to happen, and right now I needed to get to Florence. I was worried about my mom and Claire, even though my dad had said they were fine. I'd had no answer to my text messages of the day before.

I sighed and picked up the pace. Nonna Maria might be old, but she sure wasn't slow. In a few minutes, the train station came into view. I bought a ticket to Florence, and Nonna Maria and I settled onto a bench to wait.

"So tell me about yourself," Nonna Maria said.

"Um, I'm American. I live in Charleston, South Carolina," I said.

"You speak Italian beautifully."

"My dad is Italian. I've spent a lot of summers here," I answered.

My dad had said I was safe with her, and the triskelion told me she operated a safe house, but I still didn't want to reveal too much. I was becoming suspicious of everyone I encountered. I still suspected Heather the flight attendant of trying to herd me into the arms of the Velathri.

This question thing could go both ways, though. "What about you? Have you always lived in Italy?"

"No," she said. "But I have lived here for many years now, and I consider it my home."

Well, that wasn't very informative. I tried to examine Nonna Maria out of the corner of my eye. Vampire? Garda? She looked old, but she moved like a much younger person. Her hair was silver and her eyes were green. Like Johan's. I felt like a hand had grabbed my heart and squeezed. I realized I missed Johan's calm, steady presence. I hoped he'd get to Montepulciano soon.

I heard a whistle in the distance, and I felt, then heard, the rumble of the train. We stood up. Nonna

Maria took my face in both of her hands, looking deep into my eyes.

"Be safe, Mia Bella," she said, kissing me on each cheek.

"Thank you, Nonna," I replied, kissing her cheeks in return.

I turned and boarded the car that had stopped in front of me. *Florence, here I come*, I thought. I found an empty window seat and settled myself in. Early on a Saturday morning, the cars were nearly empty. A young couple with a toddler took seats at one end of the car. An elderly man read a newspaper at the other end. No one else entered, and in a few minutes, a whistle blew and the train jerked into motion. I looked out of the window for a while, watching the outskirts of Rome give way to countryside. Eventually, I pulled out *Rulers of Ireland*. Maybe I could figure out what I was doing here.

The list of rulers and their heirs seemed endless. There was someone named Fergus the Fierce who seemed important. And Dagda. And something about a cauldron that was never empty. And a spear and a sword and a stone. I yawned. Reading on a moving train had made me sleepy. I dozed fitfully, noticing when the train stopped and people got on and off, but not really waking up. Eventually, I realized I was hungry. I sat up and unwrapped the second sandwich, washing it down with a bottle of water I'd bought at the airport the day before.

A group of middle school kids on a field trip entered at the next stop. The laughing, talking students filled the seats around me. A teacher sat down beside me, which was a good thing, because when the scruffy looking man in the dark coat came in, the car was full. I slumped down in my seat, pretending to look out the window and trying to look like I fit in with the younger kids. Was it the same guy from the airport? He glanced around, not noticing me in the group of school kids, and headed to the next car. The dark, musty smell I recognized from the airport left with him. Sheesh.

What good was it to be a vampire (or half-vampire) if your parents had kept you in the dark about it and you didn't know how to protect yourself? Especially when you were something the Velathri feared and despised? I appreciated my parents giving me a "normal" childhood, but right now, a few mad ninja skills would be really helpful. I sighed. At least in Italy, I could blend in. The kids around me all had tan skin, dark eyes and dark hair, too. And they were dressed in jeans and t-shirts, just like me, and most of them carried backpacks.

I looked at my map. There was one more stop before the main Florence train station, Santa Maria Novella. With luck, the school group was headed there, too. The students were rowdy. Someone had brought a soccer ball, and several boys were throwing it the length of the train. Girls giggled and squealed, and a paper airplane soared over my head. I smiled. Vampire or not, I didn't think the guy would come into this car again. My luck held. As the train pulled into the station in Florence, the teachers began corralling their charges. Students gathered their cell phones, books, and papers, shoving them in backpacks.

"Clean up your trash! Don't leave a mess," the teacher beside me instructed.

I ducked down and picked up a paper airplane as the scruffy man in the next car peered into mine one more time. I waited, watching as he exited the train. He took up a position inside a coffee shop, picking up a newspaper and pretending to read it. I looked around for my dad. He was at a newsstand across from the coffee shop. My dad watched the passengers exit the train with a worried expression on his face. I stayed with the school group as we got off the train. Because I was taller than most of them, I kept pace with the teacher. She was too distracted by her energetic, excited charges to notice me. As we drew level with my dad, I peeled off into the newsstand.

"Katie," he said with relief. "I didn't see you get off the train."

"Hopefully, that guy didn't either," I said, nodding toward the coffee shop.

My dad drew in a sharp breath. "Let's get out of here. Now," he said, grabbing my elbow and steering me toward an exit. "My car is parked out front."

Dad didn't drive a shiny new sports car like members of the Cullen family, the wealthy vampires in *Twilight*. No, he drove an old Range Rover covered in dust. What kind of vampire was he, anyway? Oh, wait. The college professor kind. I sighed. Just my luck. We were both quiet as Dad maneuvered through Florence's afternoon traffic. Soon we were outside the city, winding our way through the narrow country roads that would take us to Montepulciano.

I had so many questions I didn't know where to start. I hadn't seen my dad in nearly a year—it felt rude to start right in with, "So, I hear you're a vampire."

I studied him out of the corner of my eye. He was handsome, with curly black hair, dark eyes, and smile lines at the corners of his eyes. He wore khaki pants, work boots, a lightweight cotton shirt, and a khaki vest. There was a beat-up khaki field hat between us on the seat of the Range Rover. It was what he always wore when he was on a dig. He looked the same as ever.

He glanced over at me.

"What are you thinking?"

"Um. That you don't look much like a vampire."

He laughed. "Well, vampires are just like other creatures. We all look different to some extent."

"And I don't feel much like a vampire."

"That's because you haven't reached your seventeenth birthday yet."

"It's in two weeks," I reminded him.

"I know. That's why I wanted you in Montepulciano this summer."

"Okay. I guess that'll be question number one. Explain why that's so important."

Dad's face suddenly went from smiling to serious. "Because we suspect your gifts will be greater due to your Garda heritage."

"But how do you know I'll become a vampire and not a Garda?"

"We don't. You could be like your Uncle Alex, and become a Garda with vampiric tendencies, or you could become a vampire with Garda tendencies.

But for several reasons, I suspect you will become a vampire."

"But don't I get to choose?"

"No. Only vampire-human children get a choice, and they choose between magic and no magic. As both of your parents are magical, you will become either a vampire or a Garda. And you need to be here when it happens."

"Wouldn't Charleston be safer?"

"No, Montepulciano is the only city on Earth that the Velathri cannot enter. Just as we cannot enter Volterra."

"What do you mean?"

"We have an agreement. Volterra belongs to the Velathri, and Montepulciano belongs to the Stregoni Benefici."

I thought that over. "So I'm safe in Montepulciano?"

"As long as you stay inside the city walls, yes."

"That's good, because I'm getting really tired of having to run from these guys. They've been trailing me since Charleston."

Dad looked stunned.

"They shouldn't know you exist," he said.

"Maybe it's not me they're after," I said flatly. "Maybe it's the book."

"What book?"

"The one in my backpack. *Rulers of Ireland*," I said.

"How did you get that book? Edward and Juliana were supposed to carry it from Charleston. Not you," he said angrily.

"It picked me. The others were afraid it would disappear again if one of them carried it, so I have it," I explained.

"That damned witch," he said under his breath.

"What?" I asked, not sure I'd heard him correctly.

"Nothing," he said, looking in his rearview mirror. "If the Velathri are after the book, they'll try to intercept us before we reach Montepulciano. We'll have to change our plans."

"Um, what does that mean?"

"It means we're taking a detour," he said, turning suddenly onto a narrow lane that didn't look wide enough for a horse, much less a car. He maneuvered the Range Rover down the uneven, winding track, stopping about two miles in. He left it running, jumping out to stand beside a large rock in front of a hill. "You can drive, right?" he asked.

"Of course, Dad," I said, rolling my eyes. "I am almost seventeen."

"When I move the rock, drive into the cave behind it."

What? He slammed the driver's side door before I could stutter out the question that formed in my mind. Move the rock? Was he crazy? I began to wonder if being tired affected your hearing.

I shrugged and moved over into the driver's seat. When I looked up from fastening my seat belt, the rock had been pushed aside and a narrow opening revealed. How had he done that? Oh, right. Vampire super strength. It was so weird to think about my dad like that. I put the Range Rover in gear and drove slowly into the cavern in front of me. As I entered, I heard the sound of the rock scraping back into place. I cut the engine and turned around in time to see my dad dusting off his hands and rolling down his shirtsleeves. Would I be super strong, too? In just two weeks? I smiled. Being a vampire might not be too bad, after all.

"Okay, Katie, let's run," Dad said.

"What about my suitcase?"

"Leave it for now. We'll get it later. Put anything you'll need right now into your backpack."

Clean underwear, socks, jeans, and a t-shirt. Make-up case. The book that had caused all the trouble. That was all that would fit. It was heavy. That super vampire strength would be welcome right about now.

"Give me the backpack," Dad said. "And follow me."

He headed toward the back of the cave, where a tunnel curved off into the dark. I took off after him, jogging to catch up.

"We need to move fast," Dad said. "Can you see?"

I realized that I could, even though the only light came from a small penlight Dad was carrying.

"Yeah, no problem," I answered. Being able to glow would come in handy right about now. Could I do it? I concentrated, willing light to pour out of my skin, but I was still just boring old me. Guess the penlight would have to do. Dad started off at a jog, and I followed. He led me through winding passages connecting a series of caverns. Eventually, the passages and caves began to look manmade rather than natural. Dirt floors and stone walls became tile, with wooden beams crisscrossing the ceiling.

Finally, we entered what looked like a wine cellar. We'd been jogging for thirty minutes, or about five miles, I estimated.

"Where are we?" I asked, looking around.

"In my wine cellar," Dad said, smiling. "You did a good job of keeping up."

"I run cross-country, remember?" I answered.

"I'm glad," he said. "And now, we're inside the city walls. Come upstairs. I'll show you your room."

We went up narrow wooden stairs that opened into a walk-in pantry off of a large, airy kitchen. I looked around. The floors were wooden and the counters were tile. Brightly colored flowers wound their way across a painted tile backsplash that covered two walls. To the side, there was an old wooden table with benches down either side instead of chairs. I was in my grandparents' house—the house I'd spent my summers in before my parents divorced. I closed my eyes and took a deep breath. It smelled the same. If I listened closely, I could almost hear my grandmother's quick, light footsteps coming down the hallway. I opened my eyes. No Nonna or Papa.

To my left, a door led outside, and to the right, another door led to a hallway. The dark wooden floors continued down the hall and into a sitting room. There were two rooms on the right side of the hallway—bedrooms. On the left side of the hallway, one bathroom. The biggest room in the house was the kitchen. The wine cellar was bigger than the bedroom Dad led me to. The white ruffled bedspread on the narrow single bed and white eyelet curtains told me he'd gone shopping before I arrived. I realized I was dirty and sweaty and tired. And really, really hungry.

"I'll make you some dinner while you get cleaned up," Dad said.

I looked at him sharply. "Can you read my mind?" I mean, maybe vampires could do that. It's not like I'd been given a lot of information so far.

"Not so much your mind as your body language," he answered, smiling. "You've had a pretty stressful journey. Take a hot shower and you'll feel better."

He was right. The shower did help. So did putting on clean clothes. I hoped there was a washing machine somewhere that I'd missed on my first look around. Yes—there it was, in a closet beside the bathroom. I knew someone who dug in the dirt all day had to have a way to wash clothes.

The smell of tomato sauce drifted down the hall from the kitchen. I headed that way, stopping in the doorway to breathe deeply.

"That's Nonna's recipe, isn't it?" I asked.

"It is," Dad said, smiling. He set a plate of lasagna on the table, adding a green salad and loaf of Italian bread. "Eat up."

He sat down across from me, a can of tomato juice in his hand. I looked at it.

"In two weeks, will I still want to eat food?" I asked, hoping the answer was yes as I took a bite of the steaming pasta dish. Melted mozzarella dripped from my fork.

Dad smiled. "Vampires can eat food. We just don't get nutrition from it. Or at least, not enough," he said.

"So … do you ever hunt?" I asked hesitantly.

"Of course."

"People?" I squeaked.

"No, of course not, Katie," my dad said patiently. "That's the point of Stregoni Benefici—to protect humans from the vampires who would use them as prey. But I do hunt animals from time to time."

I must have looked a little sick, because he continued, putting his hand over mine, "Katie, it's a part of who I am. Who *we* are. We are predators, just like the lion, or even Willow, your cat. She hunts squirrels and moles and mice. You don't think less of her for that, do you?"

I thought it over. "I guess it makes more sense when you put it that way," I said.

"I know you've been raised to think of yourself as human. And I suppose you are, to a certain extent. But you are also a vampire. And vampires hunt."

I looked down at the plate of lasagna in front of me. "What about garlic?"

"What about it?" Dad looked puzzled.

"I thought vampires didn't like garlic—or that it harmed them."

Dad started to laugh. He laughed so hard I was afraid he was going to choke. Finally, when he could speak again, he said, "Katie, we may be vampires, but we're also Italian. If garlic bothered us, we'd be in real trouble!"

Then he started to laugh again. I guess that answered that question. At least I wouldn't have to change Grandma Fiero's recipe after my birthday.

CHAPTER ELEVEN

11

I finished my meal and sat there while Dad, still chuckling, washed the plate and put it in the drain rack. Apparently dishwashers weren't in every kitchen here in Italy like they were in the US. I'd never noticed that when I was a little kid. Finally, Dad sat back down.

"I believe you have more questions?"

"I do. So many, I don't know where to start." I pressed my hands to my temples, trying to organize my thoughts. "First, when do I get my suitcase?"

"Tonight. I've sent someone for it already," he said.

"Who?"

"Marc. One of my co-workers."

That was easy enough. What else?

"How do you and Mom and the Corbetts and the Meyers know each other?" I asked. "Start at the beginning."

"The beginning is a long time ago," he said, looking at me seriously. "Because our association begins not with us, but with our parents. And really, even before them. But it's time you know."

He took a deep breath.

"About five hundred years ago, the Velathri had nearly wiped out the Stregoni Benefici in Italy.

Most of us had scattered, immigrating to other countries in Europe, or the United States and Canada. We didn't dare live together in groups for fear of drawing attention to ourselves. One group of Stregoni Benefici was able to thrive. They had fled to Ireland and remained safe for several generations. But eventually, the Velathri found them. In desperation, Fergus the Fierce, head of the Irish Stregoni Benefici, approached the Tuatha de Danann and proposed a collaboration. An alliance, if you will."

"Wait! Claire told me about the Tuatha de Danann—she said they're her cousins," I interrupted.

"Yes," Dad said. "They are, and yours as well. But I'll get to that. Both groups called the Velathri enemies, although the Tuatha had never considered Stregoni Benefici allies. We were just more vampires to them. However, the Tuatha Council heard Fergus out, and agreed that a merger would be beneficial. The two groups began working together to contain the Velathri."

He paused and took a sip of blood.

"Eventually, some vampires and Tuatha married. Your grandmother married your Uncle Alex's father when she was young. Alex's father was killed by the Velathri when Alex was a baby. Your grandmother and Alex lived in hiding until Alex reached seventeen. The Velathri lost interest when he didn't become a vampire. Your grandmother eventually married a fellow Tuatha—your grandfather."

"But what about the Garda? How do they fit in?" I asked.

"Some of the Tuatha rejected the treaty with the Stregoni. They retreated into the hidden areas of Ireland. Those who remained above ground living among humans began calling themselves Garda. Fergus and the Garda Council hoped there would be many Stregoni-Garda children born, strengthening the bond between the two groups. But so far, in five hundred years, there have been only two. Your Uncle Alex and you."

"So why have I never met him before?"

"He was born one hundred years before your mother and raised in Europe," Dad said. "Your mother was born after your grandparents left Europe for the United States. Alex was an adult by then. He's Claire's husband, by the way."

So Claire was my *aunt*? Okay, angry didn't even begin to describe what I was feeling right now. Claire had kept so much from me. And I'd told her every thought in my head. Suddenly, I remembered Johan hugging me good-bye. This brought me to my next question.

"What about the Meyers?"

"They're old friends of mine. They were already in Charleston when your mom and I married, and when we divorced, I asked them to keep an eye on the two of you," he said. "Luckily, Juliana and your mom had become good friends during our marriage and stayed friends after it ended."

"How much does Johan know?" I asked.

"Oh, he knows everything," Dad said. "He was raised in a vampire family. His parents had to teach him to blend in from the time he could talk."

"He knows everything about *me*?" I asked, feeling the anger beginning to boil again.

"I'm sure he does. Otherwise, how could he help his parents protect you?"

Oh, goody. Everyone knew everything except me! I was steaming now.

"Dad, I know you think you were doing the right thing by keeping this from me," I said, trying to keep my voice from shaking. "But you really put me in a lot of danger. And now I'm playing catch-up while the Velathri try to keep me from turning seventeen."

He had the grace to look ashamed.

"I'm sorry, Mia Bella," he said, trying to placate me by using my childhood nickname. "But your mother insisted. We didn't know if you would become Garda or vampire, and she wanted you to have a normal childhood. At the time, it seemed like a good idea."

"So tell me. How do I protect myself?"

"You spend the next two weeks inside the city walls, learning about your heritage."

"Does that include learning how to fight?"

"Yes, it does, although your mother won't like it."

"Well, I don't like having black bags put over my head at the airport and not having any way to defend myself," I said. "What if Claire and my mom hadn't been there?"

"But they were," my dad said. "And now you're here."

I opened my mouth to argue, but yawned in spite of myself.

"Go to bed now. Your training begins tomorrow."

I stood up, stretching. I really was tired. I leaned over and kissed Dad on top of his head.

"I'm sorry I got so mad. It's just frustrating—and scary—to know so little," I said.

He smiled. "I know. But that's changing. Goodnight, Mia Bella."

I fell asleep quickly, but my dreams kept me tossing and turning. I saw dark men in black coats creeping through underground passages. I saw my mother, glowing like Claire had outside of our house. And I saw my father, bleeding and lifeless on the floor of the wine cellar.

I sat up with a start. The sun was streaming through the lacy white curtains, and the smell of eggs and bacon drifted down the hall. My suitcase was lying open on top of the chest at the foot of my bed. Wonderful. Clean clothes. I shook my head, banishing the bad dreams from my mind. I got up, pulling on shorts and a t-shirt. I ran a comb through my hair, pulling it into a ponytail. I didn't know what one wore for vampire school, but I figured I needed to be comfortable for the fighting part. I tied my running shoes and walked down the hall to the kitchen. Dad was putting a plate on the table.

"Eat up," he smiled. "Your tutor will be here soon."

As I swallowed the last bite, there was a knock at the door. I heard voices as Dad let the visitor in. I turned from putting my glass and dish in the sink just in time to see the most beautiful man I'd ever laid eyes on walk into the kitchen. He looked just a few years older than me, maybe twenty-one or twenty-two, with dark hair and eyes and tan skin like mine. His face was narrow, with chiseled features, severe even. His profile would have been at home on a Roman coin. He smiled, transforming his face. I tried to breathe.

"Katie, meet Marc, your tutor," Dad said.

What? My tutor was a male model, not some old gray-bearded professor friend of my dad's?

"Ciao, Katie," the male model said. "I'm so pleased to meet you."

"Um, hi," I said, brilliantly. I looked down. Marc was holding out a package. As my hands appeared to be glued to my sides, Dad took it and handed it to me. "What is it?" I asked, certain Marc had already decided I was mentally deficient.

"Your fighting clothes. Go change," Dad said.

Fighting clothes? There were fighting clothes? I took the package to the small bedroom, closing the door behind me. Inside was a pair of black pants and a black shirt in some kind of stretchy material. Underneath them was a pair of black shoes that looked like cross-country track shoes without the cleats. I pulled on the pants and shirt. How had Marc known my size? The shoes fit, too.

I looked in the mirror. I no longer looked like an American teenager on vacation. I looked older. Mysterious, maybe even dangerous. So not me! I laughed, rolling my eyes at how silly it all seemed. Now it was time to see if Marc could actually make me dangerous. I certainly hoped so, as I really did want to live to see my seventeenth birthday.

I walked out, joining my dad and Marc in the kitchen. Dad looked at me silently, a touch of sadness on his face.

"You look grown up, Katie," he said. "Okay, you two. Off you go. I'll be at the dig all day. Just let yourself in if you get back before I do. The door's always open."

I followed Marc out of the front door and looked around curiously. I hadn't been here since the summer I was seven, but it didn't look like anything had changed. We turned right onto a narrow winding street that paralleled the city wall. The street was cobblestone, and the houses were small. As we walked, the cobblestones gave way to pavement and the houses grew larger, going from two-story to three-story, while the yards grew smaller. All of them had window boxes full of geraniums. Even the tiniest yards were full of colorful flowers. Mothers pushed strollers toward the park in the center of town, and businessmen hurried by on their way to work.

"Where are we going?" I asked.

"We usually practice at a facility outside of the city walls," Marc said. "But as you can't safely leave, I've gotten permission to use the school gym. It's summer vacation and there are no classes right now. We can also use the library to help you learn the history of your people."

More history. What happened to my summer vacation? I sighed. At least I wouldn't be tested on it. I hoped. Was there a written test to become a vampire?

We walked up the Corso, the main street leading to the city center. We stopped at a limestone building across from the park. We were proud of our history in Charleston, but three hundred years is just a drop in the bucket to Montepulciano. The earliest settlement on the site was believed to date back to 300 BC, built by an Etruscan king. The original portion of the school building was at least five hundred years old, although newer wings had been added about a hundred years ago, and a thoroughly modern gym sat out of sight at the other end, enclosing a grass courtyard where students could sit on benches under the trees to eat their lunches. Native limestone had been used to construct both old and new parts of the building, so ancient merged with modern without too much jarring of the senses.

I looked over at Marc's perfect profile as we walked. I wondered if he was a vampire or just one of my dad's students. Or both.

"How long have you been in Montepulciano?" I asked, trying to make small talk and get the answers to my questions.

"A few years," Marc answered briefly.

"So you're not just here for the dig, then," I said.

"No."

"How long have you known my dad?"

"Since I was a teenager."

Since he might be twenty and he might be two hundred, that didn't tell me much. Jeez, it was like pulling teeth to get this guy to talk. I gave up and just concentrated on keeping up with his long strides. It was a beautiful, sunny day. It wasn't hot yet, but I could tell it would be. No one had looked twice at our black outfits—strange garb for a summer day, but maybe not in the home town of the Stregoni Benefici.

Marc led me toward the school's gym. He took out a key and unlocked a side door. Inside, it looked like any other school gym. There were locker rooms, bleachers, and soccer goals. To the side I could see a weight room and another room with a padded floor and walls. Marc led me toward the room with the padding.

"Okay, now tell me what you know," he said, turning toward me.

The guy really wasn't much for small talk, it seemed. Or maybe he was just rude.

"About what?"

"About fighting."

"Nothing. I run cross-country. I'm fast. But I don't fight."

"Okay," he sighed. "So we start from the ground up."

He went to a closet and pulled out masks, padded chest guards, and fencing swords.

"Oh!" I said. "I've taken fencing. My mother made me. I never thought of it as fighting, though. It was just something to keep me busy after school while she taught. I thought you meant karate or judo."

"Good," he said, looking relieved. "Because if you're going to fight for your life, it'll be easier if the basics are already in place. And just so you know, the Italian martial arts, or fencing, is much more ancient than karate or judo."

I rolled my eyes. Another history lesson. And it appeared my mother hadn't enrolled me in fencing classes just to keep me busy while she was teaching. I'd actually been learning "Italian martial arts." Between the whole "Garda as best friend" thing and now this, I was seeing a side of her I hadn't known existed. A secretive, calculating side.

Marc and I suited up and took our stances. I felt confident. I was good at fencing. Johan and I had taken lessons together starting in first grade. Mr. Hay, our instructor, had to pair us up because no one else was quick enough to spar with us.

Before I'd even finished bowing, my sword was flying across the room.

"Hey!" I said.

"Dispense with the niceties, Katie," Marc said, handing me my weapon. "We're dealing in survival here, not a high school match."

I stood on guard, watching him warily. Two seconds later, I was disarmed again.

"Focus, Katie," he said. "Stop thinking so much. Don't analyze. Just move."

Behind the mask and padded clothes, he looked just like Johan. That was it. I would pretend I was sparring with Johan, not male model Marc. And I had never let Johan beat me. I relaxed my shoulders and bent my knees slightly. When he came at me this time, I was ready for him.

"Better," he said. "Keep going."

An hour later, I had parried most of his lunges, made two of my own, and only been disarmed once more. I was sweating and panting when he called a halt to the lesson.

"Okay. I can work with this," he said, pulling my ponytail playfully. "You may survive yet."

"That's not funny," I said.

"I know," he said, his face becoming serious. "But you've survived so far, just by using your brains. With a little more training, I think you'll be okay. Now let's get some lunch."

We stashed the fencing gear in the closet and walked to the town square. Marc led me to a café with outdoor tables, choosing one near the street.

"When's the last time you were in Montepulciano?" he asked.

"The summer I was seven," I said. "I didn't realize how much I'd missed it."

"It's your home," Marc said. "It's a part of you."

"Charleston is my home. And Montepulciano isn't the same without my grandparents."

"Montepulciano has been your family's home for centuries."

"Maybe so, but it still feels unreal to me," I said.

"I know. But it is real. You are a vampire. Not just any vampire, but Stregoni Benefici."

"But I don't feel like it!" I said, frustration showing in my face.

"You will," Marc replied, patting my hand.

"Who is this?" a woman's voice said in Italian.

I looked up to see a beautiful woman with flowing red hair standing beside our table. She wore a green dress, impossibly high heels, and a haughty look on her face.

Marc stood up. "Natalia, this is Katie Fiero, Tony's daughter," he said in English. "Katie, Natalia."

I smiled and nodded. She glanced at me with the same expression on her face that I had when I found a roach in my bedroom in Charleston, and turned back to Marc.

"Ah, the daughter of my dear Anthony. The mysterious Katherine."

She continued to speak in Italian. I narrowed my eyes. Now how did she know my full name? And why did she call Dad "my dear Anthony?"

"I'm training Katie," Marc said, switching to Italian. "Join us for lunch?"

"No, dearest, I must watch my figure. Although I am dying to know Katherine better," she said, turning cold eyes on me.

I smiled, replying in Italian, "I would love that. Come over some evening. You can tell me how you know my dad."

"Oh, you speak Italian," she said. "I didn't expect that!"

"I am Italian," I replied, my voice as artificially friendly as hers.

Marc snickered, hiding it with a cough. He sat back down and the woman in green waved good-bye as the waiter came over to take our orders. I wondered how she could navigate the cobblestones in those heels, much less make it look easy.

"Who was that?" I asked after we'd ordered. "What a witch."

Marc laughed out loud this time.

"Wait. You mean she really *is* a witch?" I said.

"Yes, she is," he said, wiping his eyes.

Why was everything I said so humorous to the people around me? I was getting tired of this.

"And what, exactly, does that mean?" I said, glaring at Marc.

"Well, it means you can't trust her," He said. "Even if she helps you, the help will come with a price."

"Like a book that disappears and reappears in a different place?"

"Yes, exactly like that," he said, his smile disappearing. "What book?"

I froze. Should I answer that? I barely knew him. What should I do? Make something up? Marc sat silently while these thoughts ran through my mind ... and across my face.

"Um, no book in particular. Just an example."

He smiled. Whoa. The smile turned handsome into stunning.

"You can trust me, you know," he said.

"How do I know that?"

"For one, your dad trusts me."

I nodded, giving him that.

"And for another, your grandparents raised me."

I looked at him, my eyebrows raised.

"You aren't another uncle or cousin I don't know about, are you?" I asked suspiciously.

"No, I'm not related to you. Your grandparents raised me after my parents were killed by the Velathri," he said. "So I have two reasons to keep you safe. The debt I owe your grandparents, and the revenge I owe the Velathri."

"I understand the debt part. But I don't get the revenge part," I said.

"There is a prediction. A prophecy if you will. That the child of a Stregoni Benefici and a Garda will end the Velathri's rule. Why do you think only two of you survive?"

"My dad said only two of us were born," I said.

Marc looked down, thinking. Speaking carefully, he said, "I'm going to tell you the truth. Your dad was trying to protect you. But the time of protection is past. It's time for you to know everything. More have been born. But the Velathri have killed all except two—Alex and you."

"Why?" I whispered.

"Alex, because your grandmother successfully kept him hidden in Ireland until he turned seventeen and he became a Garda. He is not the one so they leave him alone. You? Because your parents were successful in keeping your full parentage a secret. Until yesterday, the Velathri thought your mother was human and that you would remain human when you turned seventeen. But now, they know differently."

"No. Why did they kill the other children?"

"Because they have ruled for millennia, and plan to continue. Power. Control. It's that simple."

I cleared my throat. "How?"

It seemed I could only squeak out one word at a time, but he understood what I meant this time.

"Your mother fought alongside Claire at the airport to contain the man who tried to abduct you. When she did that, she showed what she really is," Marc said. "She did it to keep you safe, if that makes a difference. Everything your parents have done was to keep you safe."

I took a deep breath. I was supposed to be the answer to a prophecy. About vampires. Really? Up until three days ago, I'd thought I was just a regular teenage girl, looking forward to summer break and a pedicure with her best friend.

"Why did the Velathri kill your parents?"

"My mother was half-Garda," Marc said. "My dad tried to protect her, so they killed him, too."

I sat silently for a minute. "I'm sorry," I finally said.

"If it hadn't been for your grandparents, I might not have survived," Marc said. "I'm only a quarter Garda, but ..." He cleared his throat. "So, what book?" he said, changing the subject.

"Okay, you trusted me with the truth. I'll trust you. My dad has found two books during his excavations over the years," I said. "I have one of them with me. *Rulers of Ireland*."

Marc drew in his breath. "And the other?"

"*A History of Vampires*. Adam and Ariel have it."

"Garda," he said.

"Yes. It was given to the Garda for safe-keeping. They're bringing it to Montepulciano," I said.

"You believe this."

"Yes, of course. Why wouldn't I?"

"Because the Garda don't completely trust us. And we don't completely trust them."

Supernatural politics. I was finally beginning to understand what William, the book-selling werewolf, had been talking about.

"But Claire is my best friend!"

"No, she is an ancient being who protects others. And who does not trust vampires," Marc said.

"So why did she protect me?" I asked, indignantly.

"Because you are half-Garda. Because you are her niece. And because she was ordered to."

"I don't believe you," I said, folding my arms across my chest. But I did. I knew he was right. I just didn't want to admit it. We didn't speak as the waiter arrived with our food. We ate in silence, not meeting each other's eyes. Finally, Marc spoke again.

"Katie, I know this is hard. Your parents have kept you wrapped in a soft cocoon, safe from unpleasantness. The truth is hard. And sometimes difficult. But it is the truth. I promised your grandparents I would keep you safe. And I don't believe that keeping you ignorant keeps you safe."

"So how did my grandparents die?"

At some point in the past few days, I'd realized that my father's parents hadn't died of old age. Not if they were vampires.

"The Velathri. They wanted to know where you were. That's why your parents divorced. After your grandparents were killed, your dad realized he needed to distance himself from you and your mother. The Velathri were convinced. If he was willing to leave you, then you couldn't possibly be important."

I looked at him. Suddenly he was a lot more talkative, and I didn't like what he had to say.

"Don't pull your punches," I said.

"Katie, I need to know what you're made of," he said. "If you can't take it, then you might as well just walk outside of the city walls and let the Velathri kill you right now."

"Gee, thanks for telling me."

"I thought your dad would have told you that," Marc said.

"No, he's told me very little."

Marc sighed.

"I can tell. I'm afraid both of your parents still see you as a little girl. I'll walk you around the boundary on our way back."

"Growing up fast here," I said.

"Good," he replied. "Now let's go to the library."

12

He didn't mean the school library. He took me to the city library. The building was even more ancient than the school, at least eight hundred years old. The stained glass windows made it look like a cathedral inside. As it had been part of a cathedral originally, I suppose that wasn't so surprising. We went downstairs, to the rare books room. Marc showed his ID, and the librarian unlocked the door and let us in. He took down a large leather-bound volume, handwritten and hand-illustrated. He handed me a pair of white cotton gloves.

"We wear gloves to protect the pages from the oils on our skin," he said.

I put them on and turned the pages slowly, watching the history of vampires in Europe unfold in front of me. The book was mostly drawings, with the occasional phrase in Latin, which Marc translated for me. The most important part was the prophecy, which strangely enough, was written in English. I looked questioningly at Marc. He shrugged.

"No one knows when this book was written, or by whom," he said.

"Then why does everyone take it so seriously?" I asked.

"Read it."

Child of Darkness, Child of Light;
One consumes, one burns bright.
Fates intertwine, paths cross at last;
Reshape the future from the past.

"Darkness is vampire and light is Garda?" I asked.

"Yes," Marc replied.

"Huh. That doesn't sound so bad," I said. "It doesn't necessarily mean that a Stregoni-Garda child will end the Velathri's rule. In fact, it doesn't even mention the Velathri."

"That's not how the Velathri have chosen to interpret it," Marc said. "One thing that's clear, though, is that this person brings change to the established order."

"So they've killed all these children based on their interpretation of some ancient rhyme," I said. "What if they're wrong?"

"They don't really care. As long as they're in power, and remain in power, they don't care who they hurt. Or kill," Marc said. "Either way, it's worked so far."

I thought of the children who had died. I thought of Marc's parents, and my grandparents. More than ever, I appreciated my parents' efforts to keep me safe. I might not be the answer to the prophecy. In fact, I really didn't think I was. But I refused to let these guys kill more people. Starting with me.

I turned to Marc. "So what do I do?"

"First? Learn to fight. Ready to go back to work?"

Back to the gym we went. We spent another two hours sparring before we stopped for the day.

"Keep it up," Marc said. "You just might survive."

"Gee, thanks," I said, wiping my face with a towel.

"Tomorrow, we move to the dagger and the staff."

"The what and the what?"

"You need to know how to fight up close. That's the dagger. And you need to know how to grab whatever's at hand—that's the staff. Don't think you'll always have a sword when you need it," Marc said.

I sighed. Staying alive was turning into a lot of work. We walked back toward my dad's house in silence. As we walked past a tourist information office, Marc stopped.

"Let's go in here," he said. "We need a map of the city for you."

Inside the small office, Marc looked carefully at the maps.

"Here," he said, pulling one out of the pile. He paid the woman sitting behind the counter, and we continued our walk around the city's edge, where the original city walls still stood. My dad's house backed up to the boundary I couldn't safely cross. At the front door, Marc bowed, kissing my hand.

"I thought we were dispensing with the niceties," I said.

"Touché," he laughed. "See you tomorrow."

"Katie?" my dad said as I entered the house. He'd gotten back before I had. That was a first.

"It's me!" I called as I walked down the hallway to my room. "I'm going to shower and change, okay?"

"Sure, fine," he called.

I took off the black outfit and took a hot shower. I put on the t-shirt and shorts I'd started out in that morning, and headed to the kitchen. Johan and his parents were sitting at the table.

"Katie," Johan said, standing up and reaching for me. I ran into his hug. It felt so comfortable, so familiar to be in his arms. I leaned my head on his shoulder, so happy and relieved to see him I didn't even think about the fact that my dad and Johan's parents were in the room.

"Katie?"

I jumped back, letting go of Johan so fast I stumbled.

"Dad?"

"How was your training?" Dad asked, looking from Johan to me. Johan's face flamed red, and I'm sure mine did the same.

I tried to gather my thoughts.

"Fine," I said. "I learned a lot."

I didn't feel it was necessary to tell him that I'd learned he was still keeping secrets from me. I was grateful to Marc for telling me the truth, even if it had been hard to hear.

"Great," Dad said, still eyeing Johan. "Dinner's ready."

We sat down to another of my grandmother's recipes—shrimp scampi, Italian style. Everyone enjoyed it, although everyone except me drank "tomato juice" with their meals.

"So where's Mom? And Claire? And her parents … I mean Adam and Ariel?" I asked as we cleaned up the kitchen.

"They're on their way," Edward said. I didn't miss the sympathetic look Juliana gave me.

"What are you not telling me?"

Juliana raised her eyebrows and turned toward my dad.

Dad sighed. "We're not sure what's happening," he said. "Your mother should have already been here. I can't imagine what's keeping her."

"Can't you?" Edward asked sharply.

"Yes, she is Garda, but Katie is her daughter," Dad said, his own voice tense.

Edward turned to me. "Adam, Ariel, and Claire took the other book to Rome for safekeeping. We think your mother may have gone with them."

"But weren't we supposed to bring both books here?" I asked. "And why Rome?"

"Because that's where the Garda Council is located," Dad answered.

"Really?" I asked. "What about Ireland?"

"The Council moved from Ireland to Rome at the height of the Roman Empire," Dad answered. "They felt it was important to be at the center of civilization."

I thought for a minute. "So why would they take the book to the Council, rather than bringing it here?"

Dad sighed. "Because, Katie, the Council is rethinking its treaty with the Stregoni Benefici."

"What does that mean?"

"It means that if there is a war between the Velathri and the Stregoni Benefici, the Garda will sit it out."

"That's bad, isn't it?"

"Yes, Katie, very bad. One of the reasons there hasn't been all-out war before this was that with the Garda as our allies, the balance of power was in our favor."

"So, what changed?"

"Fergus the Fierce is missing."

"Um, wouldn't he be dead by now?" I asked, confused. I thought the story Dad had told me took place hundreds of years ago.

"Katie, vampires don't die of old age," my dad reminded me.

"Oh, right." I thought for a minute. "So do you think someone—or something—killed him?"

"We hope not," Adam answered. "We hope he's in hiding. But right now, we don't know. And the Garda don't know, either. Since they made the original agreement with him, they're reconsidering it now that he's missing."

"And what about the book?" I asked.

"I'm not sure what they plan to do with that. One of us will have to travel to Rome to speak with them," Dad said.

"I'm leaving tomorrow," Juliana said. "I've been friends with Libby since before Katie and Johan were born. I need to find out about the book, but I also need to make sure she's safe."

"Johan and I will stay here," Edward said.

I looked around at my dad's small house. "Where will everyone sleep?"

Edward laughed. "We own the house next door. We're not moving in with you!"

That was good to hear, because five people in this house would be close quarters. There were two bedrooms downstairs, and a large room upstairs that used to be my grandmother's sewing room, but now was my dad's home office. And then there was the one bathroom. I loved Italy, but there were some modern American conveniences I missed—like multiple bathrooms in a house. And dishwashers. And air conditioning.

"Johan will take classes with you, and I'll help your dad at his dig," Edward said.

"What exactly are you looking for?" I asked. "You already found the two books."

Dad looked uncomfortable. Apparently I wasn't supposed to go there.

I narrowed my eyes at him. "Dad?"

"There's supposed to be a third book," Dad said. "The book you have gives a history of fairies in Ireland. The book Claire has is a history of vampires. There have been rumors throughout time of a third book, which outlines a new order."

"Tell me the whole story, Dad. I can handle it."

"Okay. Legend has it that the third book, when joined with the other two on a specific date, will give us the ability to create a new world order—one where the Velathri don't rule all magical creatures by fear, one where children of fairies and vampires don't have to be hidden to survive to adulthood, one where werewolves and witches and fairies don't have to hide, living in forests and small villages and underground, so the Velathri don't hunt them down and kill them."

"I thought the books were all in Pompeii at the same time," I said.

"They were," Dad answered. "But I guess it wasn't time yet."

"You know the date?"

"Again, it's just legend. But the date predicted is the summer solstice the year the new leader turns seventeen."

"Who's the new leader?"

"That's not clear," Dad said, grimacing. "The Velathri think it has something to do with the rhyme Marc showed you today, and that's why they've worked so hard to make sure the children of fairies and vampires don't survive. Sadly, those children might have united us even without a third book, if they'd been allowed to live."

"So the Tuatha didn't—don't—trust vampires. And apparently for good reason," I said.

My dad nodded.

"So … why are they okay with you having the books?"

"I have the skills to find the books, and I promised to make copies, so each group—Garda, Tuatha, Velathri, and Stregoni—have a set," Dad said. "This means power is balanced, and no one group has an advantage. But the Garda apparently have decided to take things into their own hands."

"It's okay, though, right?" I said. "You were going to give them the book anyway."

"It's not okay," Edward said. "The originals are supposed to be kept in Charleston, in the college's rare book collection."

"I contacted the Velathri as soon as I found the first book," Dad said. "I asked permission to have copies printed. I received permission last week, which is why I asked Claire to bring it to Italy."

"You asked their permission? Why?" My brows drew together as I tried to figure that one out.

Dad sighed. "Because, Katie, the Velathri are, for lack of a better word, our bosses."

"But I thought you were here to control them. To keep them from harming humans."

"In a way. The Velathri make the rules. And they are very strict about enforcing them. The Stregoni Benifici are here to make sure the Velathri follow the rules."

I stared at him blankly. He looked thoughtful.

"Okay. Let me try to explain in human terms. I guess you could say we're kind of like game wardens. We protect the game in our forests from hunters, but we still answer to the government that appointed us, even if members of that government are hunters themselves. Does that make sense?"

Wow. This was all more complicated than I'd thought. Suddenly, I remembered something. I thought back to the conversation in my mom's kitchen the last night we spent in Charleston. It was only three days ago, but it felt like a lifetime.

"Wait. Adam and Ariel didn't know Claire had the book until three days ago," I said. "She had it hidden in her closet."

"Hmm. I wonder if Adam and Ariel took it from her," Edward said.

"Why didn't they take the book I have, too?" I asked.

"Because it has a spell on it," Juliana said, smiling. "Remember? It chose you. If they'd taken it, it would have just disappeared again."

I jumped up. "Let me give it to you now, Dad," I said. "I really don't like having it in my backpack, even if we are inside the city walls."

I went to my room and dug the book out of the bottom of my backpack. I looked down at the book in my hand as I handed it to Dad. Such a small thing to cause so much trouble.

"So we have the Garda's book, and they have the Velathri's book. This feels like a stand-off."

Dad frowned. "Both the Garda and the Velathri agreed. I don't understand what's happening now."

I was relieved to have the book out of my possession.

"Why didn't you ask me for it earlier?" I asked Dad.

"Because," he smiled. "The spell means you have to give it to me freely, without prompting. Otherwise, it just disappears again."

"Even if you're the rightful owner?"

"Even if I'm the rightful owner."

"Who put the spell on it?"

"A woman I know here in town."

I narrowed my eyes. "Her name wouldn't be Natalia, would it?" I asked.

My dad raised his eyebrows. "How do you know Natalia?"

"She stopped and said 'hi' today when Marc and I were eating lunch at the plaza," I said. "She seemed to know you really well."

"Who's Marc?" Johan asked at the same time my dad said, "Not really."

"Marc is my—I guess our—tutor," I said to Johan.

"Why were you eating lunch together?" he asked.

I stared at him. "Because it was lunch time," I said.

What was wrong with Johan? But I had more important things to worry about. I turned back to my dad.

"Really?" I asked him, going back to Natalia.

"Really," he said. "I asked her to cast a spell that would keep the book out of the wrong hands. And of course I paid her. Witches don't work for free. I didn't mention you. I didn't say I was taking the book to Charleston. I have no idea how she bound it to you."

"She almost got me killed," I said. "The Velathri might not have even noticed me if I hadn't been carrying the book."

"Tony," Juliana said gently. "You should have known better than to trust a witch. Their 'help' always comes with conditions. You know that."

Dad looked frustrated. "I had no idea she even knew Katie existed. Natalia only recently moved here, and it's been ten years since Katie visited Montepulciano. I've been careful not to return, too, until last year."

"I wonder where the witch got her information," Adam said thoughtfully. "I think it's more important than ever that Juliana find out what the Garda are thinking."

"Then," Juliana said, standing up, "I need to go home and get ready. I have to leave early tomorrow to catch the train to Rome."

Edward and Johan stood, too. "We should all go," Edward said.

"I'll see you tomorrow," Johan said as he passed me.

I smiled. At least I knew I could take Johan in fencing. I stood up to go to my room.

"Wait, Katie," my dad said. "I have something for you."

I waited while he went into his bedroom, returning with a black case in his hands.

I stared. "Is that what I think it is?"

"Yes, it's a laptop," he said, smiling. "I know you had to leave your computer in Charleston, and I thought you might miss it."

"Wow, thanks, Dad," I breathed. "It's perfect."

I opened the case, pulling out the silver laptop. I couldn't believe it. I'd thought I'd have to fight my dad for computer time on his desktop while I was in Italy."There's wireless upstairs in my study. I've already downloaded the software you need," Dad said. "All you have to do is turn it on."

"This is great," I smiled, kissing him on the cheek. "I'm going to go use it right now!"

"Don't stay up all night," Dad said, smiling. "Remember you have training in the morning."

"Right, Dad, no problem!" I answered over my shoulder as I bounced down the hall to my room. My own laptop. And the first thing I planned to do was a little research on my own mother.

CHAPTER THIRTEEN

13

I found very little. The word Garda means protector or guard in Celtic. But I already knew that. Claire had said the Garda were originally fairies, but those who wanted to live among humans had split into a separate group. I typed in "fairy." Argh. Hundreds of hits, everything from Disney's Tinkerbell to a list of gay pride parades. How would I ever sift through all of this?

Then I remembered something I had seen in the book Marc showed me at the library this afternoon. Although the book had contained a history of vampires in Europe, there had been a mention of the Garda and their treaty with Fergus the Fierce. The original Garda had been Irish, and followers of Dagda, who had been protector of his people, the Tuatha De Danann. Dagda had been mentioned in the book I'd brought from Charleston, too.

Aha, success. Dagda was known as the Celtic god of the earth, knowledge, magic, abundance, and treaties. That made sense. Dagda reportedly was skilled in combat and healing. Some versions of the story said he had a large club with two uses: one end killed, while the other end raised the dead. Other versions said he owned a large cauldron that was always full of stew, ready for company at a moment's notice. Okay, that could explain my mother's incredible hospitality. I also discovered the word Dagda means "shining divinity." And after Dagda was killed in battle, his followers, the Tuatha De Danann, a race of blond, blue-eyed people, split into two groups: those who wished to continue living among humans and those who wished to remain separate. That group disappeared into the hills and forests of Ireland and became the race known as fairies today. So the other group became Garda.

I yawned. Time for bed. I was too tired to make sense of what I'd found, but at least I knew a little more now. I was so exhausted, I didn't even dream. I was still asleep when my dad came in and shook my shoulder.

"Katie, get up," he said. "I've got to go, but your breakfast is ready. Don't keep Marc and Johan waiting."

I dug the black outfit out of the dryer, amazed when it wasn't wrinkled after sitting there all night. I brushed my teeth and pulled my hair into a ponytail. I didn't think learning to fight with a dagger was a situation that called for make-up, so I was ready. I padded barefoot into the kitchen to find a breakfast of eggs, bacon, and Italian bread laid out for me. My dad was definitely his mother's child. The idea of Cheerios for breakfast would have caused my Grandmother Fiero to go into a ten-minute spiel about how children these days didn't eat enough, didn't appreciate food, and were too skinny to be healthy. And how would you ever keep a husband happy if all you served him for breakfast was tasteless circles of cardboard with milk poured over them? I smiled at the thought of Grandmother Fiero. She'd been fierce, funny, and loving. I blinked back tears as I realized how much I missed her. The kitchen felt empty without her bustling around, entreating me to eat more.

As I finished up, there was a knock at the door. I took a deep breath. Time to learn how to defend myself. I opened the door to find Marc and Johan standing there. My breath caught in my throat. Someone had given Johan a set of the black fighting clothes, and he looked ... absolutely incredible. Gone was the slightly goofy kid I'd known my whole life. In his place was a solidly built, serious-faced young man, who was actually quite handsome. We stared at each other without speaking.

"Shoes?" Marc said, looking down at my bare feet.

"Oh, right, come in while I finish getting ready," I answered, flustered. I left them in the parlor while I went to my bedroom to grab my shoes.

"Okay, I'm ready," I said, hurrying down the hallway to find them looking at a picture of my grandparents that hung over the fireplace. It was a wedding portrait, and my grandmother looked beautiful in her Italian lace dress. Her dark hair was pulled up into an elaborate swirl that was covered by another intricate piece of lace, and her dark eyes glowed with happiness as she looked up at her handsome new husband.

"They were really special people," Marc was saying to Johan. "Katie looks amazingly like her grandmother."

I grimaced. I wasn't nearly as beautiful as she had been. But if he wanted to think I was, I wasn't going to argue.

"Okay, now to work," Marc said, leading us out of the house toward the school.

Marc and Johan walked ahead of me, talking about fencing and daggers. I rolled my eyes behind their backs. Please.

Today's workout was much harder than yesterday's had been. First, we sparred with fencing swords. Next, we practiced with daggers. Once Johan and I were reasonably proficient with them, we practiced two-against-one attacks. Marc fought the two of us off easily, but neither Johan nor I were able to stay "alive" for long when Marc was on the attacking team.

I sat on the bleachers, catching my breath while Marc and Johan sparred. I was watching their feet, trying to figure out how Marc managed to stay one step ahead of us, even when we both came at him. How did he move that fast? Suddenly, I sat up straight. I smelled something—something bad and familiar. It was the dark smell, the one I'd smelled in Rome when the guys in the dark coats were close. I'd thought it was Velathri, but the Velathri couldn't come inside the walls of Montepulciano—could they? Marc looked over at my sudden movement, and saw the expression on my face.

"Stop for a moment," he said to Johan, walking over to me.

"What is it, Katie?" he asked.

"Do you smell that?" I whispered hoarsely.

Marc sniffed the air. His face changed.

"Katie, Johan, I think we're done for the day," he said, his voice calm.

He motioned us over to the cabinet that held the weapons. Marc opened the door and held out his hand for our daggers. As he hung them on the hooks provided for that purpose, he turned a hidden knob on the wall. The back of the cabinet swung open.

"Go," he hissed.

I darted inside, and Johan followed. Marc was right behind us, closing the cabinet door and locking the back of the cabinet into place. I blinked. It was so dark the air looked solid.

"Come on," Johan whispered.

"I can't see," I said.

"That'll change on your birthday," Marc said. "But for now, let Johan lead you."

Johan grabbed my hand and pulled me along behind him. I stumbled over the uneven ground, hoping I didn't slam into anything in the dark.

"Where are we going?" I whispered.

"My house," Johan answered.

Suddenly, he stopped and dropped my hand. Metal scraped on metal, and a door opened in front of us. We were in a wine cellar like the one under my dad's house. Light filtered through the high windows lining one wall.

"Quickly, in," Marc ordered.

He turned and locked the door behind him, then barred it with a metal bar that fit into two metal hooks set into stone on either side of the door. Wow. That must be some valuable wine to protect with a door that looked like it was built to keep out monsters, I thought. Oh, wait. Maybe it *was* built to keep out monsters. We crossed to the other side of the cellar and climbed a set of stairs set against the wall. A door at the top opened into the kitchen. The cabinets and floor were a dark wood, and a round table stood in a window alcove. White lace curtains fluttered at the open window over the sink. We sank down at chairs around the table while Johan rummaged through the refrigerator. He got out two bottles of blood and one of water. He handed me the water.

"Thanks," I said, smiling at him.

I turned to Marc. "I thought the Velathri couldn't come inside the city walls."

"That wasn't a Velathri," Marc said. "That was a werewolf."

"But ... I smelled that same smell when the Velathri were after me," I said, confused. "At least, I thought it was the Velathri."

Marc looked at me sharply. "The Velathri smell like vampires," he said. "You know, like you or me."

Hmm. My forehead wrinkled as I thought about that. I smelled?

Johan grinned. "You'll be able to tell in two weeks," he said.

"You've smelled that scent before?" Marc asked me, frowning. "When?"

"At the airport in Rome," I said. "And on the train from Rome to Florence."

"Did you see the person who was following you?"

"Yeah, and he looked like Sergio, except dirtier," I said.

"Sergio?" Mark raised his eyebrows.

"A Velathri who was following us in Charleston," I said.

"Yes, I know Sergio. I'm just amazed that you do," Marc said. "And did you smell that smell when he was around?"

"No, but I wasn't looking—er, sniffing for it then," I said.

"And what led you to, um, sniff, as you put it, to begin with?"

"Well, I'd noticed that Claire, when we were walking through downtown Charleston, stopped and sniffed the air whenever she was worried," I said. "So I thought I'd try it when I got off the plane in the Rome airport. I know it sounds silly, but I was by myself and I couldn't think of a way to protect myself, and I thought it couldn't hurt and might even help ..."

My voice trailed off.

"No, that's very good," Marc said, smiling. "You did the right thing. As predators, we rely on our sense of smell quite heavily. I'm just surprised you thought to do it without training."

"So I guess that means it wasn't a Velathri who attacked me at my house," Johan said.

Marc didn't look surprised, so I guessed he'd already heard the story from Edward and Juliana.

"Your attacker smelled?" Marc said.

"Yeah. Awful," Johan answered, wrinkling his nose.

"The guy at the airport looked like he hadn't bathed in a while, either," I said. "His hair was tangled and his clothes were wrinkled and dirty."

Marc sat in silence for a moment, his face thoughtful. Finally, he spoke.

"We need to talk to your dad, Katie, and yours, too, Johan. I don't know why a werewolf followed us to the gym. They rarely ever come near a town the size of Montepulciano. They prefer big cities, where they can blend in, or forests. And the fact that one was tracking you in Rome bothers me."

He was silent again, his face thoughtful.

"Okay, we need to go to the dig. Katie, I don't think the Velathri—or the werewolves—will try anything in broad daylight in a crowd of people. Plus, Johan and I will be with you."

"Okay," Johan said, looking happy at the idea of a fight. "Let's go."

"Um, guys?" I said. "I'm hungry."

"There's no people food at my house," Johan said, grinning. "Vampires, remember?"

"Let me go next door and make a sandwich," I said. "It'll just take a minute."

"We'll come with you," Marc replied. "No going anywhere by yourself until we figure out what's going on."

"Not even my own house?"

"Not even your own house."

That was going to be a pain. We'd better figure things out quickly. The guys waited impatiently while I slapped some salami, cheese, lettuce and tomato between two slices of bread. I ate the sandwich in record time, downing a glass of milk along with it. I realized that Johan's parents had eaten all of those meals at my mom's house simply to be polite—they really didn't need the food. And of course, she's a good cook.

"Okay, I'm ready," I said, putting my dishes in the sink.

Marc and Johan were at the front door, waiting for me. My bodyguards. Fun.

"So, how do we get there?" I asked.

"We walk," Marc said. "It's only about a mile."

It was a beautiful day, with a cool breeze that offset the sun's warmth. A walk sounded fun.

"I'll go first," Marc said. "Katie, stay behind me. Johan, you bring up the rear."

Sheesh. I didn't realize this was a military operation. What happened to a walk with friends on a beautiful day through a quaint Italian town? Oh, right. Werewolves. Marc walked quickly, his head up. His eyes scanned back and forth, and I could tell he was sniffing the air around us. His body was tense, alert. Johan was so quiet behind me I looked back to make sure he was still there. The silence and tense atmosphere were getting to me. I decided to do a little more research.

"So, Marc," I said. "The Garda are fairies?"

He glanced back at me. "Kind of," he said.

"What do you mean, 'kind of'?"

"Because those who went underground became less and less like humans and more magical, while those who chose to live among humans lost some of their magic and became more human," he replied.

"But I've seen Claire glow," I said.

"The Garda still have powers," Marc replied. "And they are still protectors. But they're not as strong as they used to be. That's why I don't understand why they'd take the book and reconsider our treaty. It doesn't make sense."

"And what about the werewolves?" I asked. "Who are they loyal to?"

Marc snorted. "Themselves."

"So why are they following me?"

"As far as we know, there's just one werewolf following you. But either way, I don't know the reason. That's why we need to see Tony and Edward."

We had left my dad's neighborhood behind. Houses gave way to trees and meadows. I could see a tent in the distance, and people bent over trenches lined with string that marked the area into squares. As we approached the dig, my dad came out of a tent. He started toward us, looking angry.

"Why is she out here?" he snapped at Marc.

"There's a complication. We need to talk," Marc replied. "Where's Edward? We need him, too."

"In the tent," my dad nodded toward the tent he'd come out of. "Come on, all of you."

We ducked to enter the tent, my dad holding back the flap for us. Edward was sitting in a camp chair studying a map. He looked up, startled to see us. My dad unfolded three more chairs, motioning for us to sit down. He sat down on the cot positioned along the side of the tent.

"What's going on?" Edward asked, looking from face to face.

"Katie, you start," Marc said.

"I thought the Velathri were following me," I said. "But it might be a werewolf."

My dad and Edward hissed at the same time. It was a frightening sound, especially when combined with the looks on their faces. For the first time, they looked like predators to me. Dangerous. Monsters, even.

My dismay must have shown on my face.

"Katie, it's okay," my dad said. "I'm sorry. But the thought of you being stalked by a werewolf is …"

He took a deep breath.

"Werewolves are not our friends," Edward said. "But why are you here now?"

"There was a werewolf in the gym," Marc said.

Dad and Edward waited, their bodies still.

"We left through the weapons cabinet, taking the tunnels to your house," he said, nodding toward Edward. "But I don't know why the werewolf was there, or how he found us. And training is impossible if werewolves are following us around."

"Wait, I thought werewolves were only dangerous at the full moon," I said.

"They only change at the full moon," my dad said. "But werewolves are always dangerous. Their minds are half-animal, half-human. They don't form alliances, or at least not for long. They are unable to live in peace, even with their own kind."

"Wait, wait," I said. "What about William, the guy we met in Charleston? The bookstore owner?"

Edward smiled. "There are always exceptions. William has lived for many centuries. He's had time to reflect on how he would like to live, and he has chosen a peaceful way."

"He didn't help us, though, did he?" I asked.

"He didn't sell us out, either," Johan said.

My dad and Marc looked confused.

"There was a Velathri," I explained. "A guy named Sergio. He followed us into a bookstore in Charleston."

"Hmm. Sergio," my dad said. "He used to be a friend."

"He was outside of Libby's house," Edward said. "Juliana and I were prepared to fight him, but Claire appeared in her light form, and he left."

"Why would he be outside the house?" Dad asked. "What stopped him from going inside?"

"Adam and Ariel were inside with Libby," Edward said.

"Yes, that probably would have slowed him down some," Dad said. "But if he had wanted entrance, it wouldn't have stopped him. I wonder …"

"What about the triskelions?" I asked.

Four sets of eyes turned toward me.

"What triskelions?" my dad asked.

"The ones all over the house," I said, confused. "They're carved in stones at each doorway. And there are pictures and sculptures inside the house. It's part of mom's work …"

"They're not technically part of your mother's research," Dad said slowly. "She must have been very frightened. I wonder what of." My dad thought for a minute more. "Edward, did Sergio look angry, or did he look, perhaps, like he wanted to talk to you?"

Edward looked surprised. "I didn't have a chance to ask him what he wanted. Claire stepped in and turned on the light. You know vampires can't stand that."

"Maybe he was there to warn us," Dad said. "But Claire scared him off."

We all sat there, turning this idea over. Warn us? A Velathri? Warn us about what?

"That's an interesting theory," Edward said. "We need to find out if that's true. And we need to hear what Juliana has found in Rome. She's supposed to call me at six this evening."

Dad nodded. "Okay, come to my house for dinner tonight. For now, you three go train as hard as you can. Katie and Johan need to be able to defend themselves. As soon as possible."

"Are we safe at the gym?" Marc asked.

"I'll send friends to stand guard at the doors," Dad said. "Hold on a minute." Dad left, and I heard him calling to someone. In a minute, he stuck his head back in and said, "Kids, out here."

We walked out to find two young men standing with my dad. A young woman stood off to the side.

"This is Ben, Colin, and Adahy," Dad said. "They'll watch the gym entrances while you train."

Marc nodded. "Okay," he said. "Let's go."

I looked at Johan. "We're going to keep training?" I asked.

Johan shrugged. "I guess so," he answered.

As we followed the crowd back to the gym, I had a sudden uncomfortable thought.

"Johan," I whispered. "Um, is this safe?"

"What do you mean?"

"Is it safe for me to be surrounded by so many vampires? Don't I smell like dinner?"

Johan laughed. "No, Katie, you smell like a vampire. Already. That may be why ..."

His voice trailed off. I looked at him suspiciously. "Why what?"

He looked uncomfortable.

"Um, why the Garda decided to leave you behind."

"Johan! You're talking about my mother! She wouldn't leave me!"

"I didn't mean your mother. I meant the others. Dad thinks …" and he stopped again.

"Your dad thinks what?" I said.

"He thinks they may have forced your mother to stay in Rome with them. That's why Mom went to check on her."

"Will your mom bring her back …" this time it was my voice that trailed off as I thought of the danger to both Juliana and my mother if the rest of the Garda didn't want her to leave.

"She'll try," Johan said. "I'm sorry; I didn't mean to tell you that."

"No, I need to know. Thanks," I said, smiling briefly at him.

As we walked, I tried to think through everything I'd learned. My dad was trying to broker a new agreement—or rather, return things to the way they were before the three books were lost; each group standing alone, the balance of power equal between them. The Garda weren't happy about that, and weren't playing fair. They'd taken the Velathri's book and my mother to the Garda Council in Rome.

I was being stalked by an unkempt, smelly werewolf. Was he working alone, or for either the Garda or Velathri? Or somebody else? A Velathri councilmember had followed me in Charleston. What did he want? We had all assumed he was there to hurt me, but was it possible he'd been trying to warn us about something? And my dad hadn't known about the triskelions all over our house in Charleston. What did that mean?

We had reached the gym. Yes, we were going to keep training. Marc stationed Ben, Colin, and Adahy at the gym entrances, including the hidden one in the weapons cabinet. Marc, Johan, and I started sparring again. I felt clumsy, awkward. Marc pinned me again and again. I couldn't even hold my own against Johan.

"Johan, you're holding back," Marc yelled. "Protect Katie from my attack!"

Humph. I didn't need to be protected. I crouched, determined to pin Marc this time.

"Katie, here!" Ben tossed me a staff as Marc lunged. I swept Marc's feet from under him, leaving him on his back gasping for breath.

Colin, Adahy, and Ben broke into laughter.

"She doesn't need protection," Colin said. "She just needs a weapon."

Marc stood up slowly, rubbing his back.

"Fine. I have another idea," he said, waving Colin over. "I'm going to give you a new target, Katie."

Johan went to stand in front of the weapons cabinet while Colin and I squared off. Adahy called out instructions, allowing me to hold my own with Colin. After a while, Marc stopped our battle and had Johan spar with Ben.

I stood by Adahy, catching my breath. "Thanks," I said. "You really helped me out there."

"No problem," Adahy said. "This is a nice break from digging."

"How long have you been one of my dad's students?" I asked, taking a gulp from a water bottle and pouring some of it over my head.

"Since he started the dig. All of us are graduate assistants," Adahy said. "Your dad is one of the most respected professors in the field. We were lucky to get these positions."

"But aren't you all …" I looked around, wondering if I was crossing a line somehow by mentioning their non-human status.

"Vampires?" Adahy said. "Yes. The three of us are. Most of the workers on the dig are human. That's not why we got our positions … we really are archaeology students. But sometimes it helps your dad to have a few people around who know his secret."

"So what about, um, eating?" I asked, deciding that if I was being rude she would tell me.

Adahy laughed. "No, Katie, we don't dine on our human associates. There are plenty of deer in the woods outside the city. We take turns hunting, going one or two at a time, so nobody notices. We'll take you with us after your birthday."

Oh, ugh. I hadn't thought about that. I was still trying to adjust to the idea of drinking blood from a can labeled tomato juice. Hunting? I would go hunting? Would I even want to? As I turned that thought over, Marc called a halt to Johan and Ben's match.

"Can the three of you meet us here at nine tomorrow morning?" Marc asked our escorts.

A chorus of "Sure" and "Wouldn't miss it" came back.

"Okay, then. Class dismissed," Marc said. "I'll walk Katie and Johan back to Katie's house."

The others nodded, waving and calling "Ciao" as they headed back toward the dig, where they were living in tents like the one where we'd met with my dad and Edward. There were even separate toilet and shower tents for the men and women, and a dining hall. Everything they needed, all in canvas form.

I was glad to have met some vampires close to my own age. I realized Adahy might be able to answer some of the more embarrassing questions I had about my impending life change—things I really didn't want to discuss with my dad. Puberty was turning out to be way more complicated than I had expected.

I walked with Marc and Johan back to my dad's house, listening to them discuss the day's sparring. Tomorrow, apparently, Johan and I would get to fight off two attackers again. I yawned. While I was glad I was learning to defend myself, it was pretty tiring. I also realized I was really, really hungry. The downside of hanging around vampires, I suppose. Food—the kind I needed—didn't cross their minds. As we entered the front door, we could hear voices coming from the kitchen. I wondered who could be here as we walked down the hallway, following the sound. We found my dad and Edward. Both of them had worried looks on their faces.

"What's wrong?" I asked. "Is Mom okay? What about Juliana?"

"It's not six o'clock yet," Dad said. "Juliana will tell us what's going on when she calls. But while we wait, I've got dinner ready. Let's eat."

I filled my plate with linguine and clam sauce. Dad had salad and bread on the table already. There was water at one place, and blood at the other three. I chose the water.

"*Prost!*" my dad said, Italian for "Cheers!," when everyone was seated. The kitchen was silent for a few minutes as we all dug in. My dad was really a good cook, vampire or not. He must've learned from his mother, I thought, because this was great.

As we cleaned up the kitchen, I looked at the clock. It was 5:50 ... ten minutes until Juliana was supposed to call. Johan washed and I dried as Edward and my dad talked quietly at the table. Johan and I had figured out that volunteering to wash the dishes was a way for us to have a private conversation even with our 24/7 chaperones. Edward took out his cell phone and placed it in front of him.

"Johan," I whispered, "are you worried?"

"A little," he said quietly. "My mom can take care of herself, but this is different."

We finished the dishes and joined my dad and Edward at the table. The seconds ticked by. Two minutes to go. I stared at the phone, willing it to ring. When the sound came, we all jumped.

14

"H ello, Juliana?" Edward asked. He listened, his face serious. "So, what are you going to do? No, don't go alone. I'll come to Rome tomorrow. We'll go together."

I shifted in my seat. I looked at my dad and Johan, who seemed to be following the conversation with no problem. Apparently their vampire hearing allowed them to hear what Juliana was saying. I was the only one in the dark. Not fair. Really. Not. Fair.

"Okay. I'll be there by noon. Buy the plane tickets," Edward said. "Johan will be fine here with Anthony and Katie. He's helping Katie learn to fight. Yes, I think they're having a good time. They have an excellent instructor, and Anthony has arranged an escort for them. Three of his students. Yes, they're all vampires. And they know how to fight. Johan will be quite safe."

Johan rolled his eyes at this. I had to agree with him. I was more worried about my mom, and his, than about us. We were constantly surrounded by other people. Um, make that vampires. We were more than safe.

"I love you, too. I'll see you tomorrow," Edward said, ending the call.

"What's going on?" I asked, for the first time wishing I was already a vampire.

There was a second of silence, and then my dad spoke. "Your mom and Claire aren't in Rome. Juliana thinks they've been taken to Ireland."

"Ireland? Why Ireland?" I asked. "I thought the Garda Council was in Rome."

"It is," my dad said. "But the Tuatha de Danann are in Ireland."

"And what does that mean?"

"I don't know exactly," Dad said. "Juliana thinks the head of the Tuatha wants to speak to them."

"So are they okay?"

"For now," Dad replied. "Juliana and Edward will fly to Ireland tomorrow to make sure they stay that way."

A knock stopped me from asking my next question.

"Are you expecting anyone, Tony?" Edward asked.

"No," Dad answered shortly. "Wait here."

We sat tensely as Dad walked silently down the hallway to the front door.

"Who is it?" he asked, his voice on edge.

"It's Alex," answered a familiar voice. Dad opened the door and Alex stepped through. He sniffed. "I smell food," he said. "Is there any left? I'm famished."

"Come in," Dad said. "Yes, there's plenty. But what are you doing here?"

"I'm worried about Libby and Claire," he said as they walked toward the kitchen. "They were supposed to meet me in Rome, but they didn't show up."

"We think they may be in Ireland," Dad said. "Maybe you can shed some light on why."

Alex sat down beside Edward as Dad fixed him a plate. Between bites, Alex told us that Adam and Ariel had said they were going to get Mom and Claire and fly with them to Rome. Alex had flown ahead and waited for them at the airport. He'd been there for the past two days.

"But then I was sitting in the coffee shop, watching the gate for the next plane from Charleston, and I saw a werewolf," Alex said. "He was watching the gate, too. So I decided it wasn't safe to hang around the Rome airport and I came here. Now tell me why you think they may be in Ireland."

Edward repeated what Juliana had told him.

Alex thought for a minute. "I'll go with you. You need a Garda with you, and I spent the first one hundred years of my life in Ireland, after all."

Edward nodded. "That's an excellent idea. Two vampires in Tuatha territory will not be welcome. Your presence could help smooth the way."

Edward, Alex and Dad sat around the table talking strategy while Johan and I cleaned up the kitchen. I turned on the water full force, hoping that, combined with their own conversation, it would keep them from hearing ours.

"What do you think?" I asked. "This is getting complicated."

Johan nodded. "I'll be seventeen in two days," he said. "Then I'll have my full powers. If my dad and mom aren't back, I'm going after them."

I didn't know which question to ask first—full powers? Going after them? And I'd be seventeen in eight days. If he was going, I was, too. I decided to start with the full powers question.

"What do you mean by full powers?"

"Just as you change at age seventeen, so do I," Johan said. "As the child of two vampires, I've always been a vampire. But I'll reach my full strength at seventeen. And stop growing. I'll be mature."

Huh. Well, that was interesting. But we only had a few minutes to talk. I moved on to the next topic.

"I'll be seventeen in eight days. Wait and I'll go with you," I said.

"I can't," Johan said. "That would be too dangerous."

"Then I'll just follow you," I said. "You're forgetting my mom's there, too. And if you wait, you'll get another week of training with Marc."

We stared at each other over the dishes in the sink.

"Okay," Johan said. "If they're not back by your birthday, we'll go after them."

I glanced at the table. Dad, Edward, and Alex were still deep in conversation.

"Okay, so tell me what happens when I turn seventeen," I said.

"I don't know for sure," he said, biting his lip. "But here's what I've overheard. You'll be stronger, faster, and ... um ... thirsty."

I eyed him. "What do you mean by thirsty?"

"You'll want to hunt. Marc and I discussed this."

"You and Marc discussed me?" The adults at the table looked around as my voice rose in indignation.

"Relax," Johan said.

"Is everything all right?" my dad asked.

"Yes, Dad," I said. "We're fine."

As my dad resumed his conversation with Edward and Alex, I glared daggers at Johan. He sighed.

"We didn't think you'd want to go hunting the first time with your dad ... or mine," he said. "We thought we'd take you ourselves. Adahy and the others said they'd go, too."

Okay. Maybe I could handle this. But first I needed to ask Uncle Alex a few questions. I put the last plate in the dish rack, dried my hands, and walked over to the table. I sat down beside Alex. He and Edward were discussing flight times for tomorrow. Finally, they looked over at me.

"Alex?" I said. "How did you feel right before your seventeenth birthday?"

"Hmm. Let me think. It's been so long," he said, frowning. He clasped his hands together on the table in front of him and looked down at them.

"I remember I felt hot, then cold. And the night I turned seventeen, I woke up glowing," Alex said. "My sense of hearing, smell, and sight were much more acute. I knew that immediately. But you, I think ... will be hungry."

"Katie," my dad said. I turned toward him, my eyebrows raised. "We don't know for sure, but we think your change will be more like that of a vampire who is turned."

"What do you mean?"

"A human who is bitten and becomes a vampire," he said. "Johan was born a vampire. Alex became Garda. But you'll change from human to vampire."

"How is that different?" I asked.

"Those who are bitten fall asleep for three days. When they wake up, they're very thirsty. We don't know for sure, but just as Alex woke up glowing, we think you'll wake up thirsty at the hour of your birth and want to hunt."

Johan cleared his throat. "Marc and I will take her hunting."

It was a statement, not a question. I looked at Johan with new respect.

"And what time was I born?"

"At 3 a.m. on June 29."

It was midnight June 22. I had seven days and three hours to enjoy being purely human. Then my life as I knew it would end. I put my face in my hands.

"I'm not sure I'm ready for this," I muttered through my fingers.

My dad put his arm around me. "Mia Bella," he said. "I'm sorry this is so hard for you."

I took a deep breath and wiped the tears from my eyes.

"It's just so surprising. I wish I'd known before now …"

"Your mother and I did what we thought would be safest for you. We may have been wrong, but believe me, we were trying to do what was best."

"Okay, Dad. No more whining. I promise," I said. "And now, I'm going to sleep because I'm still a human girl and I'm tired."

The exhaustion was as much emotional as it was physical, I realized as I crawled into bed. I hoped sleep would help that, too.

CHAPTER FIFTEEN

15

The next week flew by. Marc moved in next door with Johan when Edward and Alex left for Ireland. We held a small celebration at my dad's house, complete with red velvet cake (actually flavored with blood—*yuck*), on Johan's birthday, June 24. He looked the same to me, but one thing did change—I couldn't take him down in our training sessions anymore. I lay on my back on the floor of the gym, pinned by Johan for the third time in an hour. I wasn't used to this. He grinned at me, his green eyes bright with humor.

"Gotcha," he said.

"I know, I know," I said irritably. "I give. You win, tough guy."

He rolled off of me and I sat up, rubbing my arms. We leaned into each other, back to back, as we caught our breath.

"Okay, that's enough for today," Marc said. "Katie, you've got to work harder. I can't stress how important it is that you be able to defend yourself."

"I know," I said, frustrated. "But Johan is so much stronger than he used to be."

"Then use your brains," Marc said. "The werewolves, the Velathri, and the Garda all have different strengths and skills. And we don't know who exactly is after you or if they're working together. I'm worried. Things have been too quiet this week."

He was right. We had walked to and from the gym, trained, and even spent a few evenings wandering around downtown Montepulciano like real tourists on vacation. All without seeing or hearing anything out of the ordinary. The werewolf had shown up in the gym that one time, then just disappeared.

"I know they're watching. I know they're here," Marc said. "I just don't know what they're waiting for."

"My birthday is tomorrow," I said. "Wouldn't they want to kidnap me before I change?" *Or kill me?*

Johan reached around and took my hand in his, as though he knew what I was thinking.

"That depends on who it is," Johan said. "And what they want from you."

"And that's the real problem," Marc said, sitting down beside us. "We have so many questions, and so few answers."

Colin, Ben, and Adahy walked over and sprawled beside us on the gym floor.

"We need a plan," Adahy said. "Katie turns seventeen at 3 a.m. We know she'll be thirsty. We need to take her hunting, which means going outside of the city walls. Maybe that's what they're waiting for."

Marc nodded. "We'll all go. But first, Katie, you and Johan need to know a few things about werewolves."

"I know they stink," I said.

Marc laughed. "Yes, they smell bad to us. And we smell bad to them, too."

Hmm. I hadn't thought about it from that perspective.

"Werewolves are fast, and strong, and ruthless," Marc continued. "They don't just kill to eat—they kill for the thrill of it. Or rather, the thrill of the hunt."

Yikes. Now I felt like a rabbit. A slow, tasty, and very scared rabbit.

"True wolves live and hunt in packs, cooperating and operating by a strict hierarchy," Marc said. "But werewolves are loners. They don't like rules, or laws, or order. They thrive on chaos. They prefer to live alone. And whereas the Garda and vampires have ruling councils, werewolves answer to no one— not even among their own kind," Marc said. "This is why we're having a hard time understanding why a werewolf showed up here in Montepulciano. To begin with, it's the home of the Stregoni Benefici, one of the werewolves' most feared adversaries. And it's a small city where a werewolf would definitely be noticed."

Johan cleared his throat. "I'd been doing some research into supernatural beings before we left Charleston," he said. "Werewolves like to be left alone. And in order to be left alone, sometimes they align themselves with other groups."

"I've read about this, too," Colin said. "In Ireland, sometimes the fairies use werewolves to do their dirty work."

"Exactly," Johan said. "I think the werewolf is a spy."

"For the Velathri?" I asked.

Johan shook his head. "Garda."

"But that doesn't make any sense," I said. "Claire and my mother are both Garda. My mother and I live in the same house, and Claire and I spend almost every minute together, both in and out of school. The Garda don't need a werewolf to know what I'm doing."

"I had a talk with Alex before he left for Ireland," Marc said. "He thinks the Tuatha de Danann may be the ones who hired the werewolf."

"But aren't the Garda and Tuatha de Danann the same?" I asked. "I mean, I know the Garda stayed above ground, and the Tuatha moved underground, but they're still, like, cousins or something, right?"

"It's not that simple," Marc said. "One reason the two groups separated is that the Tuatha de Danann see humans and vampires as beneath them. The Tuatha don't approve of the Garda living among humans. It would be just fine with them if a war breaks out between vampires and Garda, killing scores of us in the process. In fact, it wouldn't really be out of character for them to help that happen. And werewolves love chaos, especially the chaos created by war."

"So let me get this straight," I said. "All those children's stories about sweet, helpful fairies are lies?"

"Yes," Marc said. "In reality, they are self-centered, ruthless beings. You can't trust them."

"So when Tinkerbell tried to get Wendy killed because she was jealous of the attention Peter Pan was giving Wendy, that was totally in character?" I asked. "Wow. How did Walt Disney know that?"

"He must have met a fairy at some point," Marc said. "They can be extremely manipulative."

Colin nodded. "The Tuatha don't like the alliance between Garda and Stregoni Benefici. They think Alex is an abomination, and I'm sure they see you the same way. They've ignored Alex because he's more fairy than vampire, but it looks like you will be more vampire."

"I agree," Adahy said. "A vampire with fairy blood. I'm sure they don't like the idea of that at all."

"Why?" I asked.

Adahy shrugged. "Simple. A fairy can take down a vampire pretty easily. All it takes is a concentration of light. But you'll be invulnerable to their magic."

I remembered Claire going super nova in front of my house and Sergio leaving. So that wouldn't bother me. Interesting. Marc looked toward the door.

"It's getting dark, guys. We need to head for home," he said, looking worried. "There's a full moon tonight."

"So, that really is dangerous?" I asked.

Five heads turned toward me.

"Your parents really did keep you wrapped in bubble wrap, didn't they?" Ben said, rolling his eyes. "Yes, of course a full moon is dangerous."

"And I'm turning seventeen early tomorrow morning, when there's a full moon."

"We'll keep you safe," Marc said.

"Sounds like fun to me," Adahy grinned. "I can't think of a better birthday gift."

The walk home was quiet. Marc and Johan peeled off at Johan's house. Adahy, Colin, and Ben followed me to mine. The inside of the house was quiet. Dad was still at the dig. Adahy and I showered and changed, then started searching the kitchen for dinner ingredients as the boys cleaned up. Chicken sautéed in butter, garlic and lemon juice, served over pasta. Spinach on the side. Not bad for a thrown-together birthday dinner. Colin and Ben walked into the kitchen, sniffing appreciatively. A knock on the back door signaled the arrival of Marc and Johan. But where was Dad? I looked at Marc, my eyebrows raised.

He smiled. "Your dad will be here," he said. "Don't worry."

Just then, the front door flew open. My dad came in, arms full of balloons, roses, and the biggest dish of tiramisu I'd ever seen. My favorite dessert! He'd remembered. It would have been the best night of my life if my mother had been there. The dinner Adahy and I had thrown together was good, and the tiramisu was wonderful. And then I opened my gifts. Adahy's gift was a pair of soft leather boots.

"For running through the woods," she said, smiling.

Next, Johan handed me a small blue box. Inside was a beautiful silver locket. An intricate Celtic knot was engraved on the outside. Inside the locket was a picture of my Fiero grandparents. Tears misted my eyes as I fumbled to put it on.

"It symbolizes both sides of your lineage," Johan said as he helped me latch the chain. "Your fairy mother and your vampire father."

Ben and Colin's gift was a wooden staff. It was made of a wood I didn't recognize, with carvings of ivy winding from top to bottom.

"It's rowan wood," Colin said. "It protects the owner from evil, and so does ivy. So you're doubly protected when you carry it."

Marc's gift was a short dagger. The wooden handle was smooth, and shined to a high gloss.

"It's rowan as well," Marc said. "Keep it close."

"The boots I gave you have a dagger holder built in," Adahy said.

"Seriously?" I looked at her in surprise.

"It's time to stop thinking of yourself as a regular American teenage girl," she said. "You're not only a vampire, you're a target. We won't be able to hang with you forever, you know."

"The dagger was your grandfather's," Marc said. "He gave it to me when I turned seventeen. He would have wanted you to have it."

"Thank you," I said, tearing up again.

Finally, my dad handed me a small velvet box. I pulled off the ribbon and lifted the lid. Inside, a pair of amethyst earrings sparkled up at me. I looked up at my dad.

"They were your grandmother's," he said. "Your grandfather gave them to her when they married."

For a third time that night, I blinked back tears.

"I miss her so much," I said.

"I know," Dad said, hugging me. "I do, too."

I wiped my eyes, sniffing, and then put the earrings on. I felt warm and happy here in my grandmother's kitchen, surrounded by friends. For the first time in weeks, I wasn't worried about becoming a vampire, or being chased by werewolves. I was just happy. I examined the boots, and found the dagger sheath on the inner ankle of the left boot. It wasn't even noticeable if you didn't know to look for it. I put the dagger in the sheath and pulled on the boots. They looked silly with my khaki shorts and red T-shirt, but I knew they'd look normal—no, not just normal, but downright wicked—with my black fighting clothes.

With the amethyst earrings, Celtic locket, and rowan wood staff, I felt ready to pose for a James Bond movie poster. Or maybe *Lord of the Rings* was more like it. My dad smiled at the picture I made, standing in my grandmother's kitchen, caught between the worlds of American teenager and Italian vampire.

We all jumped as the front door banged open.

CHAPTER SIXTEEN

16

Natalia the witch blew in with a chill wind swirling around her, in spite of the fact that it was a warm June evening. She flicked her hand toward the door, which closed obediently.

"Natalia." My dad's voice was cold.

"Yes, my dear Anthony?" she asked innocently. The temperature in the kitchen seemed to drop, and I shivered.

"I wasn't invited to Katherine's party, apparently," she said, looking around at the dinner plates and wrapping paper still littering the table. "Don't you want her to have my gift, Tony?"

"You've already done enough for us, Natalia," Dad said. "A gift really isn't necessary."

"Oh, it's no trouble at all," Natalia purred. "I want her to have it."

Her smile dripped with insincerity. She reached to put a locket around my neck, but hesitated when she saw the one Johan had given me already nestled in the hollow of my throat.

"Why don't you take that old thing off and put this on?" she asked.

"Actually, Johan just gave me this," I said. "I think I'll keep it on."

A flash of anger crossed her face before Natalia controlled her emotions and smiled sweetly at me. "I'd really like to see how this looks on you," she said.

"Thank you so much," I replied. "It was really nice of you to get me a gift."

"I'm not sure this is a good idea," my dad said as I took the necklace from her. The golden locket was engraved with tiny lily of the valley flowers.

"Nonsense, Anthony. It's just a gift," Natalia said, pouting at him.

I decided the best way to get rid of her was just to put it on.

"It's lovely," I said, latching it around my neck. My dad glanced at me with a worried look on his face, but didn't stop me. The chain was delicate, but felt heavy. The locket seemed to burn slightly where it rested on my chest. I took a deep breath. Don't be stupid, I thought. Just because you don't like the woman is no reason to hate her gift.

Natalia smiled again. "I'll be going now. Enjoy your birthday!" she said gaily as she blew back out the door.

I sucked in another mouthful of air, wondering why breathing felt so difficult. Glad my ploy had worked, I reached up to unhook the locket she'd given me, fumbling with the latch.

"Let me," Marc said, stepping forward. "Ouch!" he exclaimed as he touched the chain. "The damn thing burned me!"

"It must be cursed," Adahy said. "That's why she was so anxious for Katie to put it on."

"Adahy," I gasped. "I can't breathe!"

"Don't worry, Katie," Adahy said calmly. "My grandmother was a witch. Just give me a minute."

"We don't have a minute!" my dad said, looking panicked.

"Calm down, Tony," Marc said. "First, let's get this thing off of Katie. Then, let's try to figure out who Natalia is working for, because it's probably the same person who sent the werewolf to the gym."

"Johan, hold Katie's hands," Adahy ordered. Johan sat in front of me, holding my hands as I struggled to draw air into my lungs.

"Katie, watch Johan's chest. Breathe when he breathes." I nodded, struggling to focus on the rise and fall of Johan's chest. I gripped his hands so tightly he winced.

Adahy muttered a few words, then reached out and unlatched the locket. I took a deep breath as the pressure lifted off my chest.

"Where should I put this?" Adahy asked, looking around.

"I have a rowan wood box upstairs," Dad said. "That should contain it until we can destroy it." He headed upstairs, returning with a small wooden box with a large padlock.

"Why the huge lock?" I asked.

"Because this box is made for containing evil objects," Dad answered. "Locks won't keep magic out or in, but they *will* keep curious children from opening boxes they shouldn't."

Suddenly, I saw myself as a four-year-old, finding that same box on a high shelf and trying to open it before taking it to my grandmother for help. I remembered clearly the look of horror on her face.

"Oops," I said. "I didn't know."

"And that's what the lock is for," Dad said, examining the locket before dropping it into the box and snapping the lock closed.

"That was a strong spell," Adahy said. "I think if Katie hadn't been wearing her grandmother's earrings and Johan's locket, it would have killed her immediately."

I took a deep breath, rubbing my chest where the locket had rested. A blister had formed, in a perfect oval.

"Adahy, look!" I said. "I'm blistered."

"That was definitely a killing spell," Adahy said. "Dr. Fiero, what do you know about that witch?"

My dad ran his hand through his hair, a look of frustration on his face.

"Not much," he said. "She moved here a little over a year ago. I had her put a spell on a book for me, and I paid her well for it. But that spell put Katie in danger, too."

"Where did she come from?" Ben asked.

"I don't know," Dad said. "I just came back here myself last year, when the dig started."

"I wonder," Marc said. "She speaks Italian beautifully, but there aren't that many Italians with red hair. Could she possibly have come from Ireland?"

The room was silent as we absorbed Marc's statement.

"That would mean …" my dad's voice trailed off.

"That she was sent either by the Garda or the Tuatha," Marc said. "Or both of them, working together."

I sucked in a breath.

"Mom!" I said.

"Katie, don't worry," Dad said. "She's one of them. They won't hurt her."

"But they tried to hurt me!" I said. "Why wouldn't they hurt her?"

"They tried to hurt you because of me," Dad said. "I'm sorry, sweetheart. I haven't done a very good job of protecting you."

"Tony, it's time to stop protecting her," Marc said. "She has to learn to protect herself. And Katie, that means no more accepting gifts from witches."

"You sat right there and let me take it!" I exclaimed.

"Yes, and I was wrong. I didn't think she'd try something with all of us right here. You were right when you told her you didn't want to put it on. And the rest of us should have trusted your instincts, too."

I felt drained. All the fun had gone out of the evening. Almost being killed will do that, apparently. I wanted to be alone.

"Right now, my instincts are telling me I need to sleep. So if you'll all excuse me …"

I stood and headed down the hall toward my room. I was exhausted, and my chest hurt where the locket had blistered it. I knew everyone expected me to wake up at 3 a.m., thirsty and ready to hunt, but right now I didn't see that happening.

"We'll all be here when you need us," Marc called.

"Yeah, yeah, right," I said, closing my bedroom door. I pulled on my pajamas and fell into bed. I didn't even wash my face or brush my teeth. It had been that kind of day.

17

I woke suddenly, wondering why I felt so odd. I was hungry. No, I was thirsty, the kind of thirsty that burns your throat. Moonlight poured in through my bedroom window, making the room so bright it looked like daylight. I could hear Marc and Adahy talking softly in the kitchen.

"So what did Sergio want?" Adahy asked.

"He gave Tony a warning," Marc replied. "He said to keep Katie close to home tonight."

"Are you sure that was a warning? Not a threat?"

"I trust Sergio. He and I grew up together," Marc said.

"Wait. He's Velathri. How did you grow up together?" Adahy asked.

"I was born in Volterra," Marc said. "I moved to Montepulciano after my parents died, and Tony's parents took me in."

Wait. Marc was a Velathri? And how could I hear their conversation so clearly? It was like they were in my room with me. I sat up. It was 3 a.m. on my birthday. I took a deep breath. I could smell the remnants of our dinner, wood smoke from someone's chimney, and … what was that other smell? Maybe sheep? My throat burned again, reminding me of how thirsty I was. I got up and pulled on jeans and a sweatshirt. Marc and Adahy turned toward me as I walked into the kitchen.

"Thirsty?" Marc said, handing me a can of tomato juice.

"Is this what I think it is?" I asked, examining the can.

"Yes, and I think you'll like it now," Marc said. "Did you look in the mirror before you came to the kitchen?"

"No, do I look bad?" It suddenly occurred to me that I was standing in front of one of the most beautiful men I'd ever seen, rumpled and sleepy.

"You look beautiful," Adahy said, smiling.

I wanted to look in a mirror, but my thirst was overwhelming. I took a sip of the blood. It did taste good—sweet and salty at the same time. I drained the can in about thirty seconds. Better, but still thirsty.

"We need to go hunting," Marc said. "Let's get Ben, Colin, and Johan. There's safety in numbers, and we all need to feed, anyway."

"Katie, put on your black outfit, and your new boots. Bring the dagger," Adahy said.

"Why? Will I need it for hunting?"

"No," she laughed. "All you'll need for hunting are your teeth. But you'll need the dagger for protection if anyone decides to attack us."

"Um, anyone meaning the Velathri?"

"Velathri, werewolves, Tuatha de Danann—we don't really know what we're dealing with right now," Marc said. "So we'll just be prepared for anything."

I shrugged. I felt powerful. Not afraid anymore. I'd been a fast runner before. I couldn't wait to see how fast I was now. I headed back to my bedroom to change. I looked in the mirror. I looked the same, only, somehow, better. My long dark curls were glossy, not frizzy. My skin was clear and smooth, and my lips were red and full, even without makeup. I ran my hand across the place where the locket had burned me. No blister. No redness, even.

I leaned closer to the mirror. My brown eyes were flecked with gold. Wow. Now that was interesting. I'd noticed gold flecks in Johan's green eyes before, but I'd thought that was just him. I'd have to start looking more closely at my vampire friends' eyes. Huh. Vampire friends. How weird that I hadn't even thought of that as weird.

I put on my black pants and shirt, adding the boots Adahy had given me. I pulled my hair into a ponytail, and then put on Johan's locket and my grandmother's earrings. The rowan-handled dagger was nestled in the hidden sheath on the inner ankle of the left boot. I was protected from earlobes to ankle. The boots were comfortable, a soft, broken-in leather. My footsteps were silent as I returned to the kitchen. Marc, Adahy, Ben, Colin, and Johan were waiting. Johan smiled and reached out his hand.

"Let's hunt," he said.

Marc flipped off the kitchen lights, and we headed outside. I could see even better than I had inside. I heard the breeze ruffling the leaves, and the hoot of an owl in the forest outside the city walls. I smelled the scent of the flowers growing in window boxes, the fresh water of a stream, and something I didn't recognize. Something warm that made my mouth water.

"There's a herd of deer nearby," Marc whispered. "Follow me."

We walked silently, single-file, toward the forest that lay beyond the fields behind my dad's house. My brain sorted sounds and smells so quickly I was aware of a dozen things at once: small animals scuttling away from us in the underbrush, leaves rustling around us as a slight breeze lifted them, and the warm scent of the deer in the meadow we were creeping toward. Marc motioned us forward to the edge of the clearing until we were in a line downwind from the deer.

"Watch me," he whispered. His leap was a blur as he took down the large stag at the edge of the group. The rest of the deer whirled in panic as Adahy, Ben, Colin, and Johan ran toward them. I followed, instinct and thirst taking over.

I was faster than I'd ever dreamed of being. I caught a doe with ease, biting into her jugular and drinking the warm blood without thinking. When I finished, I looked up to see the others letting their deer go. I looked down. I'd drained mine. She wouldn't be rejoining the group.

"You can drink without killing, you know," Marc said. "But you did well for the first time."

"How... how do you stop?" I asked, embarrassed.

"Don't worry," Adahy said, glaring at Marc. "It's a learned skill."

"And one we have to learn so that we don't go around leaving deer carcasses all over the place," Johan said. "People would get suspicious if we did."

"Especially when we drink from their cattle," Colin added.

"So, how do you learn to do it?"

Ben shrugged. "There's a certain amount of blood you can take from any animal without harming it," he said. "The larger the animal, the more blood that can safely be taken. It just takes practice. You'll learn."

"Thanks," I said, feeling a little better. Ben and Colin came over and dragged the carcass of my deer into the brush. "It won't be so noticeable here," Colin said. "Scavengers will take care of it."

As we turned to walk back toward the house, Marc held up his hand.

"Hear that?" he whispered.

"Yes!" Adahy hissed.

They both crouched, turning their heads back and forth, sniffing the air and listening. Ben, Colin, Johan, and I crouched behind them. Two figures skulked out of the woods, staying in the shadows at the edge of the meadow. They turned their muzzles toward us, sniffing, before loping in the direction the deer had gone.

"Wolves," I said.

"Werewolves," Marc said.

"How do you know?" I asked.

"They smell different," he answered.

I took a deep breath. The dark smell I remembered from the airport was heavy in the air. I gasped.

"They … they smell like the guy who was after me!"

"I know," Marc said. "Now we just need to figure out who sent them, and why. At least now we know there are two of them."

"And they know we're here," Adahy said. "We need to get back to the house. Now, while they're feeding."

CHAPTER EIGHTEEN

18

We ran toward my dad's house at a pace I never would have imagined before. I kept up with no problem. I wasn't even breathing hard when we pulled up in the back yard.

"Wow. I like being this fast," I said.

"I told you," Johan said, pulling on my ponytail.

"Let's get inside," Marc said, opening the back door.

My dad was sitting in the kitchen, reading a history book. He looked up, a question in his eyes. He relaxed when he saw me, putting his book down to come over and give me a hug.

"I was worried," he said. "I don't like letting my little girl go out without me."

"I was fine, Dad," I said. "Although I did kill the deer."

"You'll get the hang of it. And our metabolisms are much slower than that of humans. We don't need to eat nearly as often."

He looked at Marc. "So what's the problem?"

"We saw two werewolves in the meadow," Marc said. "They were hunting, too, so they ignored us. But that won't last."

"We need to figure out who sent them," Dad said. "Werewolves don't normally get involved in vampire politics. These two must have been hired. But by whom, and why?"

"Let's think about what we know," Marc said. "We know the werewolves have been shadowing Katie. We know the witch tried to kill her. And we know Libby and Claire were taken to Ireland, possibly against their will."

"And we know Ferdinand the Fierce is missing," I added.

"You've been paying attention," my dad said.

"Yeah, since my life is at stake I thought I should."

"Katie …"

"It's okay, Dad. You and Mom did a great job of giving me a 'normal' childhood. But I'm a big girl now."

Dad looked at me for a second, and then sighed.

"Okay. Here's what I think. I don't think it's the Velathri. They agreed to the conditions I set down when I found the first two books. Plus, they would just come after you themselves, not send werewolves. And the Garda protect humans and other beings. I think it's the Tuatha de Danann. It's like them to stay in Ireland and hire werewolves to do their dirty work."

"That's not really a surprise," Colin said, shrugging. "They never have liked our alliance with the Garda."

"Right," Adahy said, yawning. "But can we worry about that in the morning?"

"Time for us to head back to the canvas city," Ben said.

Johan and Marc headed for the front door with them.

"I'll just walk them out," I said to my dad.

When we got to the front stoop, Johan turned to Marc.

"I need to talk to Katie," he said. Marc looked from Johan's face to mine.

"Okay. I'll be next door," he said, heading for Johan's house.

"Johan," I said, turning to look up at him. His mouth came down on mine, effectively stopping my next words.

My arms crept around his neck, pulling him closer. His arms were wrapped around my waist, holding me against him. I'd been waiting for this all my life, and I hadn't even known it. His lips were soft against mine at first, and then the kiss deepened. I felt like I was melting. Finally, I pulled away.

"Johan," I said. "We need to talk!"

"I know," he said. "But we're never alone."

We stood with our arms wrapped around each other, my head resting on his chest and his chin on the top of my head.

"Johan," I whispered. "Our mothers."

"I know," he said. "We leave for Ireland tomorrow night."

"You didn't forget."

"No," he said. "I didn't."

Suddenly, a dark, dank smell hit my nostrils. I tried to push it away. All I wanted to think about was Johan's arms around me. But Johan smelled it too. His head came up, and he sniffed, looking from left to right.

"We've got company," he said.

I nodded. I didn't trust my voice at this point. We were standing at the end of the sidewalk leading from my dad's house to the street. I could smell the werewolves, but I couldn't see them. Johan turned so we were standing back to back.

"Katie," he said. "Get ready."

19

As we both crouched, prepared to fight, two wolves crept from the shrubs surrounding the fence across the street. One wolf headed toward Johan, and one toward me. As it jumped at my throat, I thrust my hand out and grabbed it by the jugular, squeezing with all my strength. I had forgotten how strong I was now. The wolf was dead in seconds. As I watched in horror, the body hanging from my hand changed from wolf to human. Shocked, I let go, and the body turned to dust as it hit the pavement. I stood frozen, tears running down my cheeks. What had I done?

"What's going on here?"

My dad and Marc were suddenly beside us, and I hadn't even seen them move. I was a failure as a vampire.

"You left them alone!" my dad roared at Marc.

Marc looked at my dad and shrugged.

"It looks like things turned out just fine."

Johan had been more successful at subduing instead of killing. I wiped tears off of my cheeks as the werewolf that Johan was still holding by the neck stopped coughing and gasping and began to breathe more normally.

"Let me go," he rasped.

"No," Marc said. "Not until you tell us who you're working for."

The man looked at each of us, hatred in his face.

"It's not worth my life."

The same words the man in the airport had said to Claire. With that, he morphed back into a wolf, squirmed from Johan's grasp and disappeared into the dark. Johan started after him, but my dad stopped him.

"Let him go. Let him tell whoever hired him that he failed," Dad said.

I turned to look at the pile of dust that had been a living, breathing entity a few minutes before. A breeze dispersed the dust as I watched. *My fault*, I thought. Marc's face was grim.

"Someone went to a lot of trouble to come after you inside of Montepulciano," he said. "Someone the wolf is afraid of."

"We know the Velathri can't enter Montepulciano," Johan said.

"True," Marc said. "However, other creatures rarely enter either Montepulciano or Volterra, because of the high concentration of vampires in both cities. Why risk it?"

"Natalia risked it," I said.

"Hmm," Dad said. "I'm beginning to think that wasn't by chance. Nor was it chance that we met the day after I found the second book."

"Let's go inside," Marc said, looking around. "You never know who might be listening."

As we turned toward the house, I realized I was shaking. I closed my eyes and took a deep breath. I leaned into my dad as he put his arm around me.

"You did great," he said. "Your grandmother would be proud of you."

I straightened up at the mention of my grandmother. "What do you mean?" I asked.

"She was one of the best fighters I've ever met," my dad said. "She taught me—and Marc—everything we know."

Wow. Sweet, dainty Nonna? A fighter? I mean, I'd always known she was tough, but wow.

I shook my head. "I've killed two beings tonight, Dad," I whispered. "I ... I wasn't prepared for that."

"No one ever is," he said. "It's one of the hardest parts of being a vampire. But you have to eat, and you were attacked and defended yourself. As a Stregoni Benefici, you have great strength and speed. You simply need to learn how to control and channel it. That's why it's so important for you to continue training with Marc."

Guilt was hitting me from all sides tonight.

"Sure, Dad," I said as I realized I would be doing no such thing.

We straggled into the kitchen. Marc and Dad settled at the table while I splashed some water on my face. Johan handed me a can of tomato juice. I looked at him.

"Drink it," he said. "It'll help."

Johan joined Marc and my dad at the table while I leaned against the kitchen counter.

"Okay, we need a list," Johan said.

"A list? Like a grocery list?" I asked.

"A 'Wants to Kill Us' list," he said. "And a 'Wants the Books' list. Then we can see if they overlap anywhere. Let's start with who might want to kill us."

"Or maybe just me," I said.

"If they go after you, they'll have to kill everyone in this room first," my dad said. "So you might as well say 'us.'"

I sighed. "This is getting much too complicated. And dangerous."

"List," Johan said. "Focus."

"Okay," Marc said. "The Velathri for one. Garda. Possibly the Tuatha de Danann."

"Witches? Werewolves?" I added, a question in my voice.

"I think they were hired by someone else," my dad said. "But that could give us a clue as to who it might be. The Velathri are not above hiring werewolves to do their dirty work. But they agreed to my proposal. And I'm pretty sure if they had an objection, Sergio would have said so. Not to mention, they would never hire a witch."

"It seems you shouldn't have, either, Dad," I reminded him.

"I know, I know," he grimaced. "I was so careful. She knows things she shouldn't."

"Like what?" I asked.

"Like you can't be killed by normal vampire-hunting methods."

"Nice," I said, smiling.

"Also," Johan interjected, "The Garda have taken the book that belongs by rights to the Velathri.

Maybe Katie isn't the real target here. Maybe it's the book."

"And where is the third book?" I asked. "Are you even looking for it, Dad?"

"Yes, Katie," he said. "That's why I've been spending so much time at the dig."

"Why do think it's there?" I asked.

"I have a letter written by the vampire who smuggled the three books out of Pompeii. He gives clues as to where he hid each of them," Dad said. "They're just not easy clues to follow."

"So what do we do first?" I asked.

"I need to find the third book. The first book belongs to the Velathri. The second book belongs to the Tuatha de Danann. We're not sure what the third book contains, but it must be really important. You and Johan need to keep training with Marc. You're doing well, but we can't let down our guard."

Johan and I looked at each other. We were going after our mothers. Tomorrow night. But we just nodded like the good kids we'd always been. Marc and Dad would find out soon enough.

I yawned.

"I thought vampires didn't need sleep," I said, surprised.

Dad smiled. "Well, first, you're only half-vampire. Also, vampires need rest, just like anyone else, and you, Mia Bella, have had a very long day."

"And night," I added, looking at the kitchen clock, which told me it was 6 a.m. The sun would be rising soon. In fact, the horizon already looked a little lighter than the rest of the sky.

"Johan and I will be next door," Marc said, standing up. "We won't practice today. I think we all need a break."

I yawned again as Marc and Johan headed for the door.

"Okay. Good night, Dad," I said. "Or rather, good morning."

"Sleep well, Mia Bella," Dad replied.

CHAPTER TWENTY

20

In my room, I checked my backpack for my passport. It was in the inside zipper pocket, where it couldn't fall out. I unloaded the dirty clothes and put in clean ones. I added my wallet, checking to make sure I had cash and a credit card. Finally, I put on my pajamas and went across the hall to wash my face and brush my teeth. I wondered if vampires had special toothpaste. "Gets the red out! No one will ever know you've been snacking on blood!" I was loopy with exhaustion. I laughed at myself and walked back across the hall to fall into bed as the sun began to rise outside my window.

When I woke up, it was light outside, but the angle of the sun was weird. I sat up, then flopped back down, remembering the night before. Of course the light looked strange—it was afternoon. I got up and walked into the kitchen. My dad had left a note. He was at the dig, and would be back by 6 p.m. I looked at the clock. It was 4 p.m. I needed to be ready to leave before he got back. I took a long, hot shower, knowing it could be a while before I had another one. I loaded dirty clothes into the washer, and turned it on. I straightened up my room, and made the bed. Then I sat down to write a note to my dad. It was hard, but eventually I wrote:

⟁⟁⟁

"Dad, I'm sorry. Johan and I are on our way to Ireland to find Mom and Julianna. We couldn't stand by and not know where they were or if they were all right. Don't worry. We're together, and Marc really has taught us a lot about defending ourselves. Love you. Katie"

⟁⟁⟁

I hid it under a book on my desk, and stood up as I heard the back door open.

"Katie?" It was Dad. I walked into the kitchen, trying to look casual.

"Have you seen Marc and Johan?"

"No. I just woke up about an hour ago," I said. "Why?"

"Well, I was going to ask them to eat dinner with us, so I knocked on their door before I came over here, but no one answered."

"Maybe they decided to get in some practice without me," I said. "I'll text Johan and see where they are."

I pulled out my phone and sent Johan a text. While I waited on an answer, I began setting the table.

"Dad, go ahead and shower," I said. "I'll let them know to come over."

My phone buzzed as Dad headed down the hall to shower.

"On the way" was all it said.

I checked the refrigerator. Hmm. Not much in there but some mozzarella and pepperoni. I realized none of us really needed to eat. We could just drink some blood and be fine. But I needed some comfort food, a reminder of my normal, pre-vampire life.

Homemade pizza had been one of my grandmother's favorites. I remembered helping her knead the dough, letting it rise, then rolling it out into circles for pizza crust when I was a child. She'd had a recipe in a box in a cabinet over the stove. I opened the cabinet, and there was the recipe box, right where she'd kept it when she was alive. I blinked back tears as I took it down. I missed her so much. I could really use her advice right now—on being a vampire, on love, on rescue missions. There was so much I'd like to ask her.

I took a deep breath and began flipping through the recipes in my grandmother's handwriting. There was the card with the recipe for pizza crust and sauce; just add shredded cheeses and toppings of your choice.

As I pulled out the card, I saw a folded piece of paper with my name on it in my grandmother's handwriting. I put the pizza recipe down and took the paper out of the recipe box with shaking hands. I unfolded it, reading through tears as my grandmother's voice echoed in my ears.

My dearest Katie—

If you're reading this, it means I'm no longer there to make pizza with you. I wish I could see you as an adult, my sweet, beautiful girl. But there is a battle coming, and your grandfather and I may not survive it. I'm leaving this letter behind your favorite recipe in hopes that one day you will return to this house and find it.

The world is full of dangers you know nothing of right now. Yet one day, you must face them. Remember: your greatest enemy is your own fear. And your greatest ally is your family's love. You are stronger than you know.

Never forget that, Nonna

I stood for a minute, listening to the sound of her voice through the years. I wiped my tears away with the back of my hand and stuffed the letter in the back pocket of my jeans. I picked up the recipe card and began pulling the ingredients out of the cabinets. Flour. Yeast. Salt. Lard. Water. I mixed the ingredients, kneading the dough into a ball, and then placed it in a bowl covered with a dishtowel to rise. As I began setting the table, my dad walked in, his hair still damp from the shower.

"So what's for dinner, Katie?" he asked.

"Pizza. Nonna's recipe."

"Mmm. I remember you loved that when you were little," Dad said. "I have a little work to finish up in the office. I'll be upstairs if you need me."

I nodded, and then turned back to cooking. While the dough was rising, I sliced a green pepper, an onion, and mushrooms. I placed a frying pan on the stove and turned on the burner. I added a little olive oil, then the vegetables. I placed a pot on the back burner and stirred in tomato paste, water, and fresh chopped basil. The scent of the cooking food filled the kitchen, reminding me again of my grandmother. I spooned the sautéed vegetables into a bowl and added crumbled Italian sausage to the frying pan.

I turned on the oven to preheat, and began to roll the dough into a circle. I pinched the edges up into a crust and brushed it with olive oil. My grandmother had always sprinkled fresh chopped basil over the crust before adding the tomato sauce. I went into the backyard and cut a few more sprigs from Nonna's garden. There. It was perfect. While the sauce simmered and the sausage browned, I took huge chunks of mozzarella and parmesan cheese from the refrigerator. I grated the cheese into a large bowl, and set it aside. It was time to build a pizza. As I turned off the stove, I heard a knock. I opened the back door to find Johan and Marc standing there.

"Wow," Marc said. "I haven't smelled *that* in years. It's your grandmother's pizza, isn't it?"

I smiled. "Yes, it is. And it's almost ready."

I layered the tomato sauce, shredded cheese, and sautéed vegetables. I drained the sausage then added it. Finally, I sprinkled more cheese and fresh basil over the top. I slid the finished product onto a pizza stone and placed it in the oven.

"That's beautiful," Johan said. "Where did you learn to do that?"

"From my grandmother," I said. "Her recipe was still in her recipe box over the stove."

"Her pizza is legendary," Marc said. "When I was in high school and my non-vampire friends came to visit, they would beg her to make it."

Dad came back into the kitchen, sniffing appreciatively.

"That brings back a lot of memories. It's so good to have you here, Katie," he said, smiling.

Guilt washed over me as I thought about what I was planning. I glanced at Johan, who was studying his shoes.

"Thanks, Dad," I said, giving him a hug. "I'm glad I'm here, too."

I looked at Johan again, who was now busily scrolling through text messages on his phone.

"Any word from your mother or your dad and Alex?" Dad asked.

"No. Nothing," Johan said, looking up. "Have you heard from Libby?"

"No," my dad sighed, running his hand through his hair. "And I'm really worried. Katie is her world. She would never have let her birthday pass without getting in touch unless something was really wrong."

He caught a glimpse of my face.

"Katie, don't worry," he said. "I'm sure she's fine. But I think Alex and Edward may be right—she may be being held against her will."

"What about Claire?" I asked. "And Adam and Ariel?"

"I don't know," Dad said. "I guess it depends on where their real loyalties lie."

Before I could ask what he meant by that, there was a scraping noise at the basement door. The basement door that led to a network of tunnels running under, into, and out of the city. We all stood frozen as the noise repeated itself.

21

S tay where you are," Marc said, placing his ear to the door. As he eased the door open, a man fell into the kitchen and lay crumpled on the floor. "Sergio," Marc gasped. "How did you ... what are you ..." his voice trailed off as the man's eyes fluttered.

"Help me," the man whispered. "I need blood."

"Yes, of course," my dad said, pulling a container from the refrigerator. He punctured the top with a straw, and then held the straw to the man's mouth. Sergio took a couple of sips, and then doubled over in pain.

"Invite me in, Tony," he rasped.

"Sergio, you are welcome in my home," Dad said. The man stretched out on the floor, taking deep breaths. He sat up, then took the container of blood from my dad's hand and finished it in three swift gulps.

"Ah, thank you, Tony," he said. "That curse is really painful."

"You know we now have the authority to kill you," Dad said.

"Yes, but I trust you won't," the man said, getting to his feet. He turned toward me. "Hello, Katie. We haven't been formally introduced. I'm Sergio," the man said, extending his hand toward me.

I took his hand and shook it briefly. It was definitely the man we'd seen outside my house in Charleston, and possibly the man who had followed us into the bookstore. I opened my mouth to ask why he was here, but Marc beat me to it.

"Why are you here, Sergio?" he asked.

"I'm here to warn you," Sergio said. "Those Garda you hang out with kept me away in Charleston, so I had to follow you here."

"Let's sit down," Dad said. "Sergio, are you hungry?"

"I could eat," Sergio said, walking toward the table.

I wasn't sure if they were talking about pizza or blood, but it turned out they meant both. My dad handed Sergio a can of blood, then put two slices of pizza on a plate and placed it in front of Sergio. He ate them in record time, and then sighed, wiping his mouth with his napkin.

"That was good. It brings back good memories," Sergio said. "So you finally learned how to make your mother's pizza, Tony?"

"No, Katie made it," Dad said, smiling. "I've never quite mastered it."

"Hmm," Sergio said thoughtfully, looking over at me. "She looks like her grandmother, too. I take it you are a vampire now?" he asked suddenly.

"Um, well, yes," I stuttered, a little offended at his abruptness. "Why do you want to know?"

"It's not just me who wants to know," he said with a smile that didn't reach his eyes. "My bosses, the

Velathri, want to know. The Garda want to know. Werewolves are roaming the woods between Volterra and Montepulciano, an area they would normally avoid. And a certain witch here in Montepulciano has been asking some very pointed questions as well. Your arrival has caused quite a stir."

"That was my fault," Dad said. "I wanted Katie here for her birthday."

"It was a good call, too," Marc said. "She needed to learn to fight. I know you thought you were protecting her by keeping her ignorant, Tony, but in reality you left her defenseless. Look how close she came to being kidnapped—twice—on her way here."

"What?" Sergio said. "Who? And Where?"

"Well, I thought ..." my voice trailed off.

"Yes?"

I sat up straight and looked him in the eye.

"I thought it was you. But now I think it may have been werewolves. I have trouble telling you apart. The long black coats, you know."

Sergio's eyebrows pulled together. His mouth turned down. I closed my eyes as I waited for him to tell me that only an idiot wouldn't be able to tell a vampire from a werewolf. Suddenly, he burst out laughing.

"Marc is right, Tony," he chortled. "You have kept her ignorant. Wrapped in tissue paper like fine china, not only hidden away from the wider world but also unaware of it." He shook with laughter again.

"I had very good reasons for doing things the way I did them," Dad said stiffly.

"I know, I know," Sergio said, the smile leaving his face. "And I can't say I blame you. Losing your parents was a shock for all of us. It must have been a difficult time for you."

"It was," Dad said shortly. "So why are you here, Sergio? We know the werewolves have been following Katie and tried to kidnap her. And we know that Natalia has tried twice to kill her. Do you have any further information? For instance, perhaps you know who is behind these attacks?"

"We have an idea," Sergio said.

"We?" I asked.

"The Velathri. We think it may be the Tuatha de Danann."

"But I thought they went underground," I said.

"Your dad finding the books changed things," Sergio said. "The Tuatha felt safe as long as the Garda had a treaty with the Stregoni Benifici. But your dad wanted to give each group copies of the books, restoring the balance of power. Which is as it should be," he said, nodding at my dad.

"However, the Tuatha like their cousins the Garda having an advantage, and they like having the Stregoni and the Velathri opposing each other. They don't want the balance restored. So they've figured out a way to subvert Tony's plan. They've taken the Velathri's book. They've taken your mother, and we believe they've taken Ferdinand the Fierce. This means they have our book, they have a member of the Garda royal family, and they have the vampire who brokered the original agreement. All they need is Katie, and they believe you will do anything to get her back," Sergio said. "Even give them the other two books."

"But he hasn't found the third book yet," I said, turning toward my dad. "Right, Dad?"

My dad sighed, a grim look on his face.

"No, I haven't. But you haven't answered our first question," Dad continued. "Why are you here, Sergio? You could have informed us of your suspicions without entering Montepulciano."

"Because we think Katie would be safer in Volterra," Sergio said. "I've come to take her back with me."

"No!" my dad and I both said at the same time.

Johan and Marc sat silently, their eyes glittering in their tense faces.

"Get up and leave before I rescind my invitation," Dad said. "You are no longer welcome here."

"Okay, okay," Sergio said, raising his hands in defeat. "I'll leave. But the bosses won't like it. And she would be safer with us. You know that."

"No, I don't know that," Dad said between gritted teeth. "Now go."

The kitchen was silent as Sergio stood up and headed for the door to the tunnels. "I warned you, Tony," he said, before opening the door and slipping through it. "Thanks for the pizza."

Marc recovered first.

"Do you really think it's the Tuatha and not the Velathri?" he asked.

"I'm not sure," Dad said, rubbing his eyes. "His story is believable, but the Velathri aren't above lying to get what they want. And wanting Katie in Volterra ..." Dad's voice trailed off.

"Dad, you're tired. Get some rest, and things will be clearer in the morning," I said.

I hoped my guilt didn't show on my face. He did look tired, and I did want him to rest. But I also wanted him to be asleep when I snuck out to meet Johan for our journey to Ireland later tonight. Very soundly asleep, because while I could be vampire quiet, he also had vampire hearing.

"You're right, Katie. Things will be clearer in the morning," Dad said as he stood up and took Sergio's plate to the sink.

"I'll do the dishes, Dad," I said, jumping up. "You go rest."

As I cleaned the kitchen, Marc and Johan discussed Sergio's visit in quiet voices.

"Um, guys?" I said, turning toward Marc and Johan. "I'm tired, too," I said, looking daggers at Johan.

"Oh, right," he said, jumping to his feet. "We'd better get some sleep, too, right, Marc?"

Marc looked from Johan to me, then shrugged and got to his feet.

"Yes, you'd better," he said, smiling. "I've got a long day of practice planned for tomorrow."

"Great," I said, "I'll see you in the morning."

I cringed at the lie as it came out of my mouth. Johan and I would be halfway to Ireland by morning. Because of Sergio's visit, we were leaving later than we'd planned. It was already midnight. Sunrise was in six hours. We needed to get moving. In my room, I double-checked my backpack. I brushed my teeth and pulled my hair into a ponytail. When I turned from the mirror, Johan was standing there.

I squeaked, smothering the sound. "A little warning, please?" I hissed.

"I'm trying not to wake your dad," he whispered back. "And put on your fighting clothes."

"Don't you think those will stand out on a train?"

"We're not taking a train. We're running. I don't want anyone to see us. We'll have to take cover at daybreak, so let's get going."

I went into the bathroom and changed into the black form-fitting outfit. I stuffed my sweatshirt, t-shirt and jeans into the backpack.

"Okay," I whispered. "Let's go."

"Do you have your necklace and earrings?" he asked.

"I'm wearing them," I said. "The boots and dagger, too."

"Good. And bring your staff," Johan said.

I had planned to leave the staff behind, thinking that it, like the black outfit, would look suspicious on a train or a plane. But if we were running ... well, the staff could only help. The last thing I did was take the note I'd written my dad out from under the book where I'd hidden it. I placed it in the center of my dresser, where he'd be sure to see it. I weighted it with a picture of me with both my parents, taken the summer before they divorced.

"Okay," I said. "Let's go."

We started out at a lope, long easy strides that wouldn't win any races, but would allow us to keep going for a long time. After two hours, we stopped at a hillock overlooking a stream to rest and drink some blood. We had to be careful because we hadn't been able to pack much in our backpacks.

"Johan, what will we do when we reach the ocean?" I said.

"Marc's family keeps a yacht in Saint-Malo, France. We'll sail to Ireland using his boat. You do remember how to sail, right?"

"You told Marc?" I gasped. "Won't he tell my father?"

"Yes, I told Marc," Johan said. "We need someone to know where we're going. And no, he won't tell your dad. He thinks your parents have protected you too much already. He promised he'd do his best to keep your dad calm tomorrow morning."

"*Why* does everyone keep secrets from me?" I asked, miffed. "And yes, of course I remember how to sail. You taught me."

Johan grinned. "I know," he said, throwing a pinecone at me. I caught it and glared at him.

"Come on," he said. "Try me."

I launched myself at him. He caught me in his arms and we rolled over and over until he stopped us at the stream's edge. His face hovered over mine.

"Katie?" he said, a question in his voice.

"Yes?" I answered, breathless both from rolling down the hill and from his nearness.

"Can I kiss you?"

I laughed. "*Now* you ask me?"

Johan sat up. "I guess that means no."

"No! I mean yes," I said. "Hang on. Let me rephrase that. Yes, I want you to kiss me. But why ask now? You kissed me the other night."

"I want to be sure of how you feel," Johan said. "I don't want you to kiss me because we've been friends forever and you're just being nice. I want you to *want* to kiss me. Does that make sense?"

I reached out and grabbed his chin, turning his face toward me. "Yes, I want to kiss you, Johan. And not as friends. Wait, I want us to be friends. But more—"

Johan's mouth on mine silenced my babbling. Based on his reaction, I was pretty sure he understood what I'd been trying to say. I wrapped my arms around him, feeling the muscles in his back ripple under my hands. Suddenly he pulled away, putting a finger over my lips.

"What?" I whispered.

"I heard something," he said, looking toward the top of the hill. I sat up, sniffing the air. The dark smell filled my nostrils.

"Werewolf," I whispered, my lips so close they grazed his ear.

22

S tay still," he hissed. We sat, barely even breathing, for what was probably just a couple of minutes, but felt like hours. Finally, we heard a twig snap as footsteps moved off into the forest. "I think it's gone," Johan whispered in my ear.

"Our backpacks! They're at the top of the hill," I whispered.

"I know," Johan said. "Move carefully. I think the sound of the stream covered our voices, but we can't depend on that when we get to the top of the hill."

We crept up the hill. My backpack was shredded, my clothes strewn on the ground under the tree where we'd stopped.

"I think he was looking for something," Johan said.

"Maybe he thought I have the book. Or books," I said.

"Well, you did leave Charleston with one of them," Johan said.

I sighed. "My backpack is ruined. You'll have to carry my clothes in yours."

"No problem," Johan said, folding my clothes into tiny squares and shoving them into an empty section of his backpack.

"Anything else?"

I searched all the pockets of my shredded backpack, making sure I hadn't missed anything. I dug out my passport and wallet and handed them to Johan. Suddenly I stood up and looked around.

"What?" Johan asked.

"My staff. It's gone."

I felt my ankle, then my neck and earlobes. Dagger, necklace and earrings still intact.

"Everything else is here. It's just the staff."

"That's bad, but we can make do without it," Johan said. "I wonder why a werewolf would want a rowan wood staff. He'd have to wear gloves to touch it."

"I don't know. Proof, maybe? That he'd found us?"

"Maybe. Let's keep moving," Johan said. "We've got to reach the yacht by daylight. Then we can rest."

I stood there, looking at him. He looked back steadily, then leaned down and brushed his lips across mine. He smiled and brushed my hair out of my eyes. I wasn't sure what to think. Johan had always been my friend and now—

"We need to go," he said. I nodded, not trusting myself to speak.

We started out again, at a faster pace this time. We had three hours at best before sunrise, and a lot of miles to cover.

The horizon was just turning pink when we ducked under the chain that was strung across the entrance to the marina at Saint-Malo. We walked down the docks, turning in at the tenth berth on the right. The boat was named Cathleen. My grandmother's name.

I looked at Johan. "Did you know the boat was named after my grandmother?" I asked.

"Cathleen was your grandmother's name?" he said, surprised.

"Yes. I'm named after her," I said.

"You are?"

"Yes. Katherine is the English version of..." My voice trailed off. Cathleen was the Irish form of Katherine. But my grandmother had been Italian.

"Cathleen is an Irish name," Johan said.

"Yes. Why did my Italian grandmother have an Irish name?"

My mother's mother had been from Ireland. Was my father's mother Irish, too?

"Another question to add to a long list," Johan said. "Let's get sailing."

We motored out of the harbor, raising the sails once we were clear. Johan set the computer-controlled pilot on a course for the south end of Ireland. Johan took first watch, and I crawled into the small bedroom space in the bow. As I closed my eyes, I fleetingly hoped Johan wasn't as tired as I was, but I was too exhausted to worry about it for long. I woke up a few hours later as Johan clambered down the hatch.

"Your turn," he said as I stretched. "I've set the automatic pilot and the radar. We're sailing for the southeastern coast of Ireland. We're too far south to be in any major shipping channels, but keep your eyes open just in case."

He opened a small refrigerator and handed me a can of tomato juice. I stared at it until it sank in that this was really blood. I yawned and rubbed my eyes, popping open the "tomato juice" and taking a swallow. It must have been on the boat for a while. It was cold, and thick, and not very good. But it cooled the thirst that burned my throat. Johan looked at me with sympathy as I grimaced.

"It's all that's available on the boat," he said. "But the forests of Ireland are full of game. The occasional goat or two isn't bad, either, I hear. Just try not to kill them."

"Right," I answered. "So what's our final destination?"

"We're headed for the Hill of Tara, in County Meath," he said. "We'll have to run some more tonight."

"Why there?"

"It's the traditional home of the High King of Ireland," Johan answered. "Now located underground."

"So how do we find the entrance? Is it marked?"

"Um, no. We go to the Stone of Destiny and wait for them to invite us in."

"Stone of Destiny? Really?"

It all sounded so ... so ... other-worldly. I mean, Charleston had its share of ghost stories. What three-hundred-year-old city didn't? But Stone of Destiny? High King of Ireland?

Johan pulled a *Fodor's Ireland* out of his backpack and handed it to me.

"It's there. Look it up," he said. "And now, it's my turn to sleep."

I took the book and headed above board. The wind was steady and the sails were set to capture its maximum power. Johan really did know what he was doing. The sun sparkled on the slightly choppy water, and a school of dolphins kept pace with the boat off to my left. It was a beautiful day—hard to believe that werewolves and power-hungry fairies would like me dead. Speaking of power-hungry fairies, I turned to the Fodor's index, and looked up County Meath, where the Hill of Tara was located. The seat of the High King of Ireland. It *was* real. And so was the Stone of Destiny. I was looking at an actual photograph. Amazing.

The Stone of Destiny was located on top of a small hill. It made perfect sense that the Tuatha de Danann lived underneath it. I examined the picture. There didn't seem to be an opening, but there was a tomb close by, called the Mound of the Hostages. That didn't sound good. Fodor's called it a Neolithic Passage Tomb. I wondered what that meant.

I put the book down and let my mind drift. Johan had always been there, a part of my life. Our mothers had been friends since before we were born. We'd been pushed down King Street side by side in strollers even before we could walk. Later, as toddlers, we'd played in either his kitchen or mine as our moms visited and drank coffee. We'd gone to school together since kindergarten. I'd always thought of him as, well, kind of like a brother. I mean, please. We went to our Junior Prom together, and he didn't even hold my hand.

But our friendship had been changed forever now. I tried to figure out how I felt about that. We were still friends, but also something more. And I decided that it felt pretty good. Like some missing part of my life had fallen into place.

The sails began to flap, and I stood up to adjust the lines. There were no other ships or boats in sight, and I knew my vision went a lot farther than it used to. I squinted. There *was* something on the horizon ahead of us. I looked at the radar—land. The sun was low on the horizon when Johan came above deck. We were within sight of Ireland—a largely uninhabited part of the coast, if the lack of lights was any indication.

"Farmland, mostly," Johan said, as if reading my mind. "The sheep won't mind if we dock here."

"How did you know about this place?" I asked.

"Your uncle, Alex," he said. "He told me where to come."

"When?" I asked. "You talked to him?"

"Before he left," Johan replied. "He thought this might happen."

I thought that over in silence. People I loved were still keeping secrets from me. What else was I going to learn? I turned to Johan, my hands on my hips.

"Johan. Stop keeping things from me. If I'm going to be helpful at all, I've got to know everything," I said. "I've learned a lot in the past month, and I haven't fallen apart yet. So tell me. Everything. Now."

He turned from tying the boat to a ramshackle dock to stare at me.

"What do you mean?" he said.

"My uncle. You didn't tell me you'd talked to him."

"I couldn't. I couldn't let your dad know he'd told me about this place. I had to keep it a secret, and we were never alone. Vampire hearing, remember?"

I sighed. "Okay. I'll give you that one. But the fact that I'm half-Garda and half-vampire?"

Johan looked uncomfortable.

"I didn't know your mother was Garda," he said. "I just knew about your dad. Keeping you in the dark was your parents' choice."

I glared at him.

"Okay, so my parents told me not to tell you, either," he mumbled, looking down as he coiled the line in his hands. "We were kids. I didn't think it mattered."

I closed my eyes, taking deep breaths.

"There's no one around to hear us now. Is there anything else I should know?"

"I ... I can't think of anything," he said, looking up. "Except ... we need to be careful. The Tuatha de Danann don't play around. And neither do the Velathri. We're here to get our mothers and Claire if she wants to come, and go home."

"Claire? You think she might not want to come?"

"I don't know. She's married to Alex, who's half-vampire, but I don't get the feeling she likes vampires very much," he said.

"Why do you say that?" I asked.

"I don't know," Johan shrugged. "Just things I've picked up on when she's visited our house to talk strategy with my parents. She acted like she hated to be there, and couldn't wait to leave."

I stood silent, realizing I needed to stop thinking of Claire as my best friend since fourth grade, instead of an ancient being who'd been given the job of guarding me as I grew up. She'd protected me when there was still a chance I might become Garda, but now that I was definitely a vampire ... I was surprised to find tears rolling down my cheeks.

I turned my back and tried to wipe them away with my hands, hoping Johan hadn't noticed. I felt his arms come around me.

"It's okay, Katie," he said. "She does love you, you know."

"I know," I said. "It's just that so many things have changed, and the person I would normally talk everything over with is Claire."

"I know it's not the same, but you can always talk to me," Johan said. "You know that, right?"

I turned around and put my arms around his waist, leaning my head on his chest.

"Yes," I replied. "And I'm glad you're still here, and still my age, and that you'll still be in school with me next year."

Johan laughed.

"If we live through the next twenty-four hours," he said.

I thought back to something else he'd said.

"When you say go home, do you mean Montepulciano or Charleston?"

"Charleston," he said with conviction.

"But Marc said Montepulciano was safer," I argued.

"There's a map," Johan said. "I think it shows that Charleston is the new seat of power. I believe Charleston is where we need to be."

"Where is it? The map?" I asked.

"In a vampire safe house outside of Dublin," Johan replied. "But first, we need to speak with some fairies."

"Okay," I said. "Let's go."

We lowered the sails and folded them into tiny triangles that fit under seats on the deck. We latched the hatches and made sure the boat was securely docked. Johan lifted his backpack onto his back. Then we stepped off of the Cathleen and headed into the forest as the sun edged below the horizon, leaving us in darkness. We jogged through the trees, sampling the air around us as we ran.

"Deer," Johan said. "Let's feed."

I agreed. The thirst was burning my throat, making it hard to think of anything else. We caught two deer unawares and emptied them both.

"I thought we weren't supposed to kill," I panted as we pulled the carcasses deeper into the woods.

"We have a long run ahead of us," Johan said. "And possibly a fight. So we need all the blood we can get."

I nodded. I felt strength flow through me as the blood entered my system.

"We'll feed again before we reach the rock," Johan said.

We started our run again, jogging north at a manageable pace. I reveled in the smooth flow of muscle over bone, the easy movement of breath in and out of my lungs. We were covering ground at an amazing pace. We ran through the night without stopping. Johan slowed, and then bent into a crouch as the sun began to peek over the horizon.

"Shh …" he said. "Sheep. And don't kill this time."

"How do I stop?" I whispered. "I don't know how. And I'm thirsty."

"Think before you drink," Johan said. "Stop. Breathe. Then bite."

We crept toward the herd, looking and listening for guard dogs. I really, really didn't want to kill a dog. That would be more than I could handle. Several sheep were sleeping on the outside edge of the herd. I watched as Johan crept forward, and then gently turned a sheep's head back. He drank from the jugular, stopping long before I would have.

That was the key, I realized. Stop before your thirst is quenched. I copied his movements, letting the sheep go after just a few swallows. I moved to the next one, drinking quickly and silently. A dog barked in the distance.

"Time to go," Johan whispered. "We need to get to the stone."

As the horizon changed from pink to gold, we stood by the Stone of Destiny. It perched on a hilltop, surrounded by grassy green fields. Sheep grazed peacefully in the distance, separated from us by low stone walls.

"Come."

The voice came from behind us. I turned, and saw a tall man with long blond hair staring at me with startlingly green eyes. He was wearing fighting clothes like ours, but when I looked closely, I could see they were dark green, not black. A short-handled dagger hung from his belt.

"Let's go," Johan said, taking my hand.

Our guide turned and led us toward the Mound of Hostages. Of course. Where else would evil fairies keep captives? In the Mound of Hostages, by the Stone of Destiny, at the Seat of the High King. Just wait until I wrote this year's "What I Did on My Summer Vacation" essay.

23

We ducked through the low doorway into the round stone entrance. The curve of a winding passageway cut off the light from outside. Soon, the dark was so complete it appeared solid, even to my vampire eyes.

"Ouch!" I said, as the dark actually became a solid wall. Suddenly, I could see Johan and our guide just fine. Both of them were staring at me, Johan with a smirk on his face and the tall blond guy with a slight frown.

"What?" I said irritably. "I bumped into the wall. Why didn't you turn on the lights sooner?"

"Katie," Johan grinned. "Nobody turned on a light."

I looked down. The light was coming from me. I was glowing. Like Claire had in the tunnels under Charleston.

"So it's true," the fairy said. "Your mother is a Garda."

"Yes, you know she is," I snapped. "And we're here to take her home."

Johan shook his head slightly, squeezing the hand he still held.

I took a deep breath. "Sorry," I said. "I'm just worried about her."

"So are we," our guide said. "Allow me to introduce myself now that we are underground. My name is Breannan."

As he spoke, he turned and placed his hand on a barely visible symbol scratched into the wall. The stone slid aside, revealing another passage that went deeper into the hill. This passage was lined with torches, making my personal light unnecessary, which was good, as I had no idea how I'd done it.

"What do you mean, you're worried about her?" I asked as Breannan's words sank in. "Isn't she here?"

"No, but Johan's mother is," Breannan said. "And your aunt and uncle," he said, looking at me. "At least we know now that they are who they say they are."

"Are you ..." my tongue suddenly felt numb. I swallowed, cleared my throat and tried again. "Are you holding them hostage?"

"No, they are here of their own free will."

Yeah, but were they free to leave? I noticed Breannan hadn't answered that question. We reached another door, this one made of rowan wood a foot thick. The familiar three swirls of the triskelion decorated the hinges and lock. We entered a large room dug out of solid rock. Torches burned around the walls, and a large fire roared in a fireplace at the other end of the room. Water trickled from a small waterfall into a stream that ran along one side of the room then exited at the back. The roar of the fire and the splashing of the water didn't hide the fact that all voices stilled when we entered. I clutched Johan's hand tighter and slid a little behind him as everyone in the room turned to stare at us.

Claire was there. And Alex and Edward and Juliana. Beautiful people who looked like Breannan, all dressed in shades of green, sat at tables scattered around the large room. And at the largest table, beside the fire, was a large man who was obviously the fairy king. He wore no crown except a twist of ivy, but his position in the room and the deference of the others told me who he was. His face was lined and his blond hair and beard were streaked with gray. His green clothes were embroidered with tendrils of ivy, and a rowan staff that looked just like mine was leaning against his chair. It *was* mine. The king smiled at the surprise on my face.

"Recognize this, young woman? I did, too, when it was brought to me. It belonged to my great-grandfather, once upon a time," he chuckled.

Wait, what? Who had brought it to him? How had Ben and Colin gotten the staff and then given it to me if it had belonged to the king's great-grandfather? And most importantly, where was my mother?

"Come, sit, and I'll answer your questions," the king said. He waved his hand, and two chairs appeared at his side. Johan and I walked forward and sat down. Breannan remained standing by the door, his hands clasped loosely behind him—a not-so-subtle reminder that we weren't going out the way we came in unless he wanted us to.

"Johan!"

Juliana started from her chair, but sank back as the king held up his hand.

"Patience, my dear," he said. "You can see he is unharmed."

"You promised," she whispered.

"Yes, I did," he said. "And now, let us hear their story."

The tension in the room made it hard to breathe. The king's green eyes boring into mine didn't help.

"When you are ready, my dear," he said.

"What do you want to know?" I asked.

"Everything. Start from the beginning. We are, as you can see, a little cut off from the rest of the world down here."

He laughed, and all the other fairies in the room laughed with him. Okay, weird. And here I thought he was going to answer *my* questions. I wasn't sure how interested he was going to be in my last day of junior year, in my not getting a pedicure because of stupid werewolves, and shopping with Claire and Johan while being stalked and robbed by a weirdo dressed as a tourist, but whatever. He'd asked.

So I started with seeing the man I now knew to be Alex entering the empty house on the way to school my last morning of being a normal teenager. I told how Johan had found the book in the school library, and then lost it. I told them about William, and Sergio, and the dark, awful smell of the werewolf in the airport. The king smiled as I told about meeting Nonna Maria on the train and going home with her.

"You know her?" I asked.

"She's my sister," he said. "She's chosen to live among humans, but we stay in touch."

That explained the triskelion I'd seen above the doorway at her house. Apparently all of these supernatural beings knew each other. It was about as bad as living in downtown Charleston, I decided.

I told them about getting to Montepulciano, learning to fight with Marc, and the werewolves who followed us into the city center. I told them about my birthday, and how the witch Natalia tried to kill me. I stumbled a little over becoming a vampire. I wasn't sure how forgiving these nature beings would be of me killing deer and cattle and sheep to feed. I got the distinct feeling they'd rather I fed on humans.

I told them about Sergio's visit, and his assertion that the Tuatha de Danann were behind the attempts of my life. A few murmurs ran through the crowd at that, but the king held up his hand and they subsided. Then I told them about sailing to Ireland and running through the night to reach the Stone of Destiny. I told them about our hope that my mother was here.

The only thing I left out was the kisses Johan and I had shared. Considering I was holding on to his hand like it was a life preserver, I thought it would be a little redundant. Besides, some things are private, even if you are the king.

"So it appears you're not a changeling," the king said. "We, um, don't always keep up with them like we should," he added, examining his fingernails.

"Changeling? What's a changeling?" I asked, confused.

"A changeling is a fairy child we leave with a human family. We trade a human baby for one of ours."

"Why would you do that?" I asked, outraged.

"Why? So that fairies have eyes and ears in the world of humans, of course," the king said, looking surprised.

"So … what happens to the human children?"

"They become our servants. Their lives are much better than they would have been above ground," he said defensively.

I'd noticed the people in light green standing against the walls during our talk. At first, I thought they were fairies too, but as I looked more closely, I saw that they were not quite as beautiful, not quite as graceful.

"But, but … they were taken from their families!" I protested.

"Not always a bad thing. Especially for humans," the king replied. "But enough of this. You want to find your mother. And now I will answer your questions. The rowan staff was lost years ago during a battle with Velathri. It has been in vampire hands ever since. A werewolf found it in the forest and brought it to me, hoping to trade it for my visitors. But that would have been very poor hospitality on my part, so I paid him in gold and sent him on his way. We are not the ones who want you dead. We would not send a witch or a werewolf," he said. "In fact, you must not believe that yourself to come here."

I suddenly realized just how much danger I'd put myself and Johan in by coming to Ireland. What if it *had* been the Tuatha who'd been trying to kill me?

"I didn't really think about it. I just wanted to find my mother."

"Understandable. But that I don't know." The king frowned. "Does that answer your questions?"

"No, I have a few more," I said, sitting up straight. "What did the werewolf want with your visitors?"

"Why, to make a meal of them, I'm sure," the king laughed. "I find vampire to be quite stringy, myself."

I wasn't sure if he was joking or not, so I moved on to my next question.

"Where is Fergus the Fierce?"

"The last time I saw him, he was well enough," the king chuckled. "He stayed a few nights with us, but said he had important business elsewhere. Let's not waste time on such topics when we have guests! I propose a feast!"

The king clapped his hands and the human servants began to bring out platters of meats and vegetables and fruits, each more colorful and aromatic than the last. I guess question-and-answer time was over. As the servants moved among the fairies, Juliana slipped into a chair beside Johan.

"Don't eat anything," she whispered under cover of the fairy band starting up. "If you do, you have to stay here forever, or at least until they decide to let you go."

As we were vampires, and didn't really need to eat, this wasn't a problem. Except the king noticed.

"You reject my hospitality?" he asked, his eyebrows raised.

Alex stood up and walked over to me, covering my hand in his.

"My niece is worried about her mother. We would like to continue our quest to find my sister," he said. "All of us."

"Ah," the king sighed. "This has been so entertaining. I have so enjoyed having visitors from the surface. You must all come again!"

He lifted his cup in a toast, and all the other fairies lifted theirs. Alex nodded at us, and we stood and walked cautiously toward the exit, where Breannan still stood.

"Breannan," the king boomed. "Escort our guests out!"

He turned to toast a beautiful woman dressed in an olive green gown. An ivy crown twisted through her waist-length red hair. The queen, it appeared. She didn't look unhappy to see us go.

24

Breannan closed the door behind us, muting the sound of revelry as we headed up the passage. No one spoke as we concentrated on moving quickly and quietly. Juliana wrapped her arms around Johan as we reached the surface.

"Mom," he muttered, looking embarrassed.

"I wasn't sure we were getting out of there alive," she said, hugging him closer.

Breannan looked at us seriously as Alex helped me through the low doorway into the daylight.

"Johan, Katie. The two of you are the keys to peace among our peoples," he said, handing me a folded piece of paper. "We have waited thousands of years for your births. Don't waste this chance."

He turned and disappeared back into the Mound of Hostages. I unfolded the paper to find a map of Charleston. But this wasn't a map for tourists. It was a map for fairies. Triskelions decorated the border. A red circle with the number three in the center was drawn where my house stood. Street names were in Celtic.

"What does that mean?" Alex asked. "What did he say to you, Katie?"

"Wait," I said. "Let me think."

Johan and I were the key? I wasn't sure what that meant. I'd figured out that our friendship wasn't random, that we hadn't grown up around the corner from each other by chance. But the key? The key to what exactly? I turned to ask Johan what he thought, but he was talking to his parents.

"We need to go," Edward said. "We don't have time to figure it out now."

We started out at a jog, running across the fields that surrounded the Stone of Destiny.

"We want to reach the forest before the sun crests the hill," Alex said. "Hurry."

As we neared the edge of the forest, a dark mist began to ooze from between the tree trunks. Claire and I froze in our tracks as Alex stopped, then began slowly backing up.

"The Velathri are here. We need to return to the Stone," Alex hissed. "We'll be safe there. They can't come near it. When I say run, turn and run … run!"

Claire and I turned and sprinted toward the Stone with Johan and his parents on our heels. We reached the Stone of Destiny in seconds. I bent over, winded.

"Alex!" Claire was looking wide-eyed in the direction we'd come.

"Isn't he right behind us?" my voice choked off as I saw what Claire was looking at.

Alex swung his dagger, slicing necks as smoky beings in dark cloaks converged on him. Heads rolled and bodies dropped, but there were too many of them. He disappeared under the onslaught. Edward and Juliana leaped to his defense, standing in front of Alex as he lay bleeding on the ground.

Claire turned into a towering column of light so bright the vampires nearest her burst into flames.

"Don't look!" Edward grabbed Juliana's face and held it to his chest.

But Edward looked straight into the light without being harmed. I turned in alarm toward Johan, but he was fine, too, if a bit stunned. How was that possible? But I had other, more pressing problems to think about right now. The dark mist parted around Edward and Juliana and spread toward us, darkening the early morning and turning dawn to twilight.

Johan and I were safe by the Stone, but how long could we stay there? Suddenly, there was a green wall between us and the dark figures emerging from the oozing mist. I watched, unable to breathe, as fairies pulled shining swords with ivy-carved rowan handles from hidden sheaths.

"You need to go," a voice said in my ear.

Breannan was standing there, the rowan staff in his hand.

"The two of you need to leave now," he said, handing the staff to Johan. We both looked at Breannan in confusion. "The king wants you to have it," he said, bowing.

"Me?" Johan said. "Doesn't it belong to Katie?"

"No, it belongs to you," Breannan said.

"Well, why didn't the king just say that while we were there?" I asked.

Breannan sighed. "Because the queen was present, and he didn't wish to upset her."

"Upset her? Why would that upset her?"

"Think, Cathleen," Breannan said, giving my name its Irish pronunciation. "Vampires don't often have green eyes. Your parents aren't the only ones who've been keeping secrets. Now go."

He turned and joined the battle, leaving me open-mouthed. Johan looked as stunned as I felt.

"Did he mean ..."

"Later," I said. "We need to go. The map says Charleston, and we're an ocean away."

I saw swords swing and heard the clash of metal on metal. Then I turned and grabbed Johan's hand, pulling him with me up the hill behind us. At the crest, we turned and looked back.

Bodies littered the hillside, and battles continued in the open fields. The rising sun glistened on the blood staining the grass of the pasture red. Black mist oozed and grasped at fairy ankles, and ivy twisted and tripped dark-cloaked Velathri. Fairies shot light from their hands, blinding vampires, and vampires ripped at the necks of the Tuatha, biting through them without effort. I stood paralyzed, watching the carnage in horror.

"Katie, come on," Johan said. This time it was his turn to pull me down the other side of the hill, away from the sights and sounds of battle.

"Where are we going?"

"The safe house. We're only a few hours away on foot."

25

We didn't stop to rest. We ran through the day, keeping to forests as much as possible. As the sun began to sit low on the horizon, I could tell we were getting close to a city. Forests gave way to fields, and I could hear the sound of cars in the distance.

"Almost there," Johan said. "We'll spend the night and fly out of Dublin early tomorrow morning."

I could see a farmhouse in the distance, surrounded by fields with both sheep and cattle grazing on the green summer grass.

"Is that where we're going?" I asked Johan.

"No, that's where the caretakers live," he said. "They take care of the safe house, and keep the herds ready for us to snack on."

"Caretakers?" I asked.

"Caretakers are humans with one supernatural parent. They're not only paid well, they're our friends," Johan said.

"So, humans aren't usually our friends?" I wondered aloud.

"No, not usually," Johan said. "They're afraid of us, and that makes them dangerous."

"Well, after meeting the Velathri, I can't say I blame them," I said.

Johan led me down a path to a cottage hidden in a copse of trees on the other side of the pasture from the farmhouse. Inside was rustic, but homey, with one large room serving as the kitchen, dining and living area. There was a bedroom and bathroom off of the living area.

"You go first," Johan said, pointing at the bathroom. "I'll buy us plane tickets online."

I felt better after a shower and a change of clothes. The house was small, a two-room cabin really, but fully stocked with everything we needed. Even WiFi. When I walked back into the living room, drying my damp hair with a towel, Johan was sitting at the computer. When he turned around, his face was serious.

"What's wrong?" I asked.

"Katie," he said, closing his eyes and taking a deep breath.

"Is my mom all right? My dad?"

"Yes, they're fine," Johan said. "It's Alex. The Tuatha tried, they really did, but it wasn't enough."

I sat down on the couch. Alex. I'd barely had time to get to know him. I sat in silence as Johan told me he'd been wounded giving us time to get to the Stone of Destiny. After the battle, the Tuatha had given him their blood, and Johan's parents had given him theirs, but he was too badly injured.

"And Claire?"

"She disappeared," Johan said. "I'm sorry, Katie. My parents are injured, plus it weakened them to give blood to Alex. They're staying with the Tuatha until they're able to travel, or they'd go after her."

I was out of tears. I'd cried them all already. I was tired, and I was angry. A cold, hard anger that focused my thinking. Framed on the wall was a larger copy of the map Breannan had given me.

"Johan, we've got to figure out what Breannan meant by us being the key. The key to what? And how?"

"Okay, you research and I'll get us some blood," Johan replied, heading toward the small kitchenette in the corner. "Start with the number three, and we'll go from there."

As I took the can from his hand, I wondered when we'd stopped calling it tomato juice. Johan headed for the shower as I pulled up Google and typed in "significance of the number three." There were all kinds of things based on the number three: the trifecta, the school trimester, and the Holy Trinity, for starters.

But apparently, three had been an important number long before Christianity came along. In Greek mythology, there were the three Furies, the three Fates, the three-headed dog Cerberus. And apparently, where oak, ash, and thorn grow, fairies live. I recognized the next symbol. It was a triskelion. It was the same symbol I'd seen carved into the rowan wood door leading to the dining hall of the fairies, and at Nonna Maria's house. And the stone doorstep of our home in Charleston. I'd stepped across it almost every day of my life.

There were three aspects to its meaning, of course: forward motion or change, for one. Secondly, it symbolized past, present, and future, which totally made sense when linked to the forward motion part.

And finally, the three worlds: other world, mortal world, celestial world. So forward motion toward the future of … the three worlds? I sat staring at the computer screen, trying to think through all the different levels of meaning contained in that one symbol.

"That symbol is in this house, too," Johan's voice came from behind me. "It's in all safe houses."

"But why?"

"Because after the Garda and the Stregoni Benefici joined forces, the Garda offered to help make safe houses safer," Johan said.

"So why is there a triskelion in my house?"

"Because your house is a safe house," Johan said.

I'd never thought before about the strangeness of seeing that symbol on my doorstep. Charleston was old—there were still cobblestone streets in a few areas—but it wasn't European old. It wasn't Celtic old.

"Think about it, Katie," Johan said. "Where did most of the stones in Charleston come from? We studied this in school."

The stones had served as ballast on ships arriving from Europe. Once the ships arrived, the stones were unloaded in Charleston so the goods of the New World could be loaded onto the ships for the return trip. Charlestonians had put the stones to good use, building roads and walkways with them. And, apparently, magical protective doorways.

"There aren't many safe houses in the United States," Johan said. "Those stones have always been difficult to smuggle out of Ireland because of their power. Charleston and Boston have a couple. There are several in Quebec City ..." His voice trailed off as he saw the look on my face. "More than you can take in right now?" he asked.

I closed my eyes, took a deep breath, and shook my head.

"I'll be okay," I said. "When's our flight?"

"Tomorrow morning at nine. We're an hour from the airport here, so we need to get up early."

I shut down the computer and stood up. I didn't feel like I'd learned anything useful. I knew the number three was important, and I understood why I'd been seeing triskelions everywhere I went. But how was that related to today's battle? What major change was coming to the three worlds? I yawned. I was too tired to figure it out right now. As I looked toward the bedroom, it sank into my exhausted, overloaded brain that there was only one bed.

Before I could react, Johan spoke. "You take the bed. I'll sleep out here on the couch."

Looking at his face, I realized he looked even worse than I felt. My uncle was dead, but both of his parents were so badly injured they couldn't even travel.

"No, it's a big bed," I said. "I don't really feel like being alone, anyway."

"Are you sure you don't mind?" he asked, looking relieved.

"Not as long as you promise to hold my hand," I said.

We fell asleep hand in hand, and it was the most peaceful night I'd had in a long time. I didn't even dream. I woke up to find I'd turned on my side during the night, and Johan was curled up behind me, his arm thrown across my waist. I sighed and laced my fingers through his, comforted by his nearness. I realized, lying there, that my entire life had been turned upside down. My dad was a vampire. My mom was a fairy. My "best friend" was really my aunt. Only Johan was who I'd always thought he was. I listened to his even breathing, wishing I could stay where I was forever—wrapped in his arms, safe, warm. I realized that without him, I would have been lost in this strange new world of fairies and vampires. Maybe even dead. I pulled his arm closer around me, shivering at the direction my thoughts had taken.

Johan stirred, and then spoke. "Flight's in three hours. Let's go."

I got ready in record time. We were going home.

26

We found a scooter and helmets in a small shed behind the house.

"Who will pick up the scooter?" I asked as we headed toward the airport.

"The people who maintain the house," Johan said.

The next twenty-four hours passed in a blur. We left the scooter in long-term parking, checked in, and boarded our plane without incident. I slept most the way to Charleston, only waking up when the stewardesses came through with warm washcloths for our faces. The sun was setting as we exited the Charleston airport. A few taxis were waiting for passengers. A city bus shuddered to a stop in front of us, brakes squealing. Johan headed for the bus.

"Johan," I said, jogging after him. "What about a taxi?"

"They're a little obvious," he said. "Buses go by all the time, and nobody notices."

The interior of the bus was dim, and smelled like dirty feet and cigarettes. Only a few people sat in the dingy seats, staring blankly out of the windows as the bus jerked into motion. Johan and I moved to the back, sitting near the rear door. I tried not to breathe too deeply as I warily eyed the people seated in front of us. No black coats. No awful werewolf smell—just awful people smells. I relaxed slightly and looked out of the window beside me. The bus took the exit for downtown Charleston and slowed, stopping at a red light at the top of Meeting Street. We got off the bus near Marion Square Park. Streetlights gleamed, lighting the residential streets around us.

"Keep to the shadows," Johan said.

We walked quickly, coming toward my house from the north. We stopped in a driveway across the street, crouching behind the cars parked there. Lights were on, and figures moved behind the curtains.

"They're home," I said, starting to stand up.

A hand reached out of the shrubbery beside me and jerked me off my feet, slamming me into the gravel of the driveway. I flipped and kicked, trying to see who had grabbed me. Johan was in a choke hold, his face turning red across from me.

"Dad?" I said, sitting up. "What are you doing?"

Dad let hold of Johan's throat, and I turned to see Marc brushing gravel from his jeans.

"Sorry," Dad whispered. "We had to stop you from going in."

"But who's in there if you're out here?" I hissed back.

"Your mother and Sergio," Marc said.

"I thought the house was a safe house," I said.

"Sergio must have been invited in," Marc said.

"What are you saying?" I demanded, my voice rising.

"Shh!' Dad whispered. "We don't know. We're trying to figure it out."

"Without getting you hurt," Marc said.

"And how are you going to do that?"

"Marc is going to sneak up to the back door and try to hear what they're saying."

"But what if Marc gets hurt?" I said, my voice rising again.

"He's smarter than that. Don't worry."

Don't worry? I was tired of being told that. I couldn't sit here and let everyone else take the risks. I'd headed for the plane when the werewolf attacked in the airport, leaving my mother and Claire to deal with him. I'd let Dad and Marc protect me in Montepulciano, and I'd let Johan take care of all of our travel plans. Johan and I had run when the battle started at the Stone of Destiny. Now it was my turn.

I crouched quietly, waiting until everyone's attention was on the house. I shifted my weight, pretending to stretch, but really moving myself back a few inches, toward the hedge behind me. No one appeared to have noticed, so I shifted again, putting my back against the hedge this time. Marc leaned over to whisper something to my Dad. Now was my chance. I rolled backward through the hedge, ending up on my feet on the other side.

I ignored the twigs in my hair and the horrified, "Katie!" I heard as I sprinted across the street toward the side yard of my house.

We were on my territory now. I had grown up here. I knew every shrub, every shadow, the way the back gate sagged so it wouldn't latch, and how to lift and push it so it swung silently in toward my backyard. Light spilled out of the open back door. Sergio stood there, looking out.

"What's wrong?" I heard my mother say. She came to stand behind him.

"I thought I heard something," Sergio replied.

I held my breath as he sniffed the air.

"Werewolf," he said.

27

Wait, what? I took a deep breath, and the dark horrible smell I knew to be werewolf filled my nose and nearly made me choke. I'd been so focused on my mom and Sergio, I'd forgotten to pay attention to what else might be creeping around in the dark with me. I froze. My mom and Sergio were safe as long as they stayed in the house. But Dad, Marc, and Johan were behind me. I needed to warn them, or maybe serve as a distraction. I stood up and strolled toward the street. I kicked a rock and watched it skitter into the gutter. I walked away from the hedge where my dad, Marc, and Johan were crouched, and headed toward East Bay Street. I sniffed. I could still smell the werewolf. My plan must be working.

I strolled casually, pretending not to notice the crouched figure keeping pace with me in the shadows. Suddenly, I heard yells behind me. I turned to see my dad and Johan grappling with two werewolves. I sprinted toward them, wondering where Marc was.

He flew out of the shadows at the same time I did. I realized Marc had been following me, not the werewolves. I was a failure as bait, but I was a good fighter, thanks to Marc's training. I pulled my dagger out of my boot, and fell on the werewolf that had Johan pinned, slitting his throat. Marc snapped the neck of the werewolf holding my dad. Their bodies fell to the ground, then turned to dust and drifted away.

"Everybody okay?" Marc said, helping my dad to his feet.

"Yeah," Johan said, pushing himself into a sitting position. "Wow, that was close. They jumped us from behind!"

"Good thing Katie paid attention in class," Marc said, reaching over to tweak my curls.

I ran my hands through my hair, pulling out twigs and leaves. My dad leaned heavily on Marc, looking drained.

"Dad? You don't look so good …" I trailed off as I saw the dark stain on his shirt. "You're bleeding. We've got to get you inside," I said. "Marc, Johan, carry him!" I ran for the front door of my house, banging on it and yelling, "Mom, open up! Now!"

Sergio opened the door, looking surprised. I didn't even stop to wonder why he was so comfortable in my house. I pushed past him, heading for the downstairs bathroom where we kept a first aid kit.

"Mom, Dad's hurt!" I yelled, running back to where Marc and Johan were lowering my dad onto the couch in the front room.

"What happened?" Mom said, coming to stand beside Sergio.

"We were jumped by some werewolves," Johan said. "I think he was bitten."

My mom gasped, putting her hands over her mouth. Sergio looked grim.

"Don't just stand there!" I yelled. "Help me!"

I unbuttoned Dad's shirt, pulling it carefully away from the wound. I grabbed alcohol and poured it over the gaping hole.

Dad hissed out a curse, and then gasped, "Katie, alcohol won't help. A werewolf bite is fatal to a vampire."

I stopped breathing for a second. I'd fought with werewolves twice now, and no one had ever told me that. No wonder vampires and werewolves didn't mingle. But that wasn't important now. What was important was my dad.

"Dad, there has to be some way. I won't let you die," I said desperately.

I looked at Sergio. "What can I do? Is there any way to save him?"

"There are legends but I've never heard of it being done," Sergio said.

"What's the legend?" I asked, placing gauze carefully on Dad's wound. It might not help, but it made me feel better to be doing something.

"That the blood of two half-breeds will cure a werewolf bite."

Marc nodded. "I've heard that, too."

I stared at them. "Two half-breeds? What are you talking about?"

"You," Sergio said. "Half-vampire, half-fairy."

"But two? Where will I find another? Alex ...."

I sucked in a breath, remembering Alex was dead.

"Johan's father lives," Sergio replied.

It was Johan's turn to look blank. "My father? What do you mean?"

"Your father is the son of the Tuatha king," Sergio said. "Why do you think you have green eyes?"

"That means ..." I thought fast. "Will Johan's blood work?"

"I don't know that anyone's blood will work," Sergio said. "It's just legend. But you can try."

"Okay, Dad," I said, turning to look at him. He was gray and still. I put my hand on his chest and felt a slight thump. "He's still alive," I said. "How will we get him to drink?"

"Use your dagger, Katie," Johan said. "Here, I'll go first."

Johan took my dagger and sliced it across his palm. He held it over my dad's mouth, letting the blood drip into his open mouth. I took the dagger and did the same. Dad didn't wake up, but pink spots appeared in his cheeks, and he began to look a little less gray. I took a deep breath and sat down on the floor beside the couch. Johan sat beside me. I put my head on his shoulder and took his hand.

"Thanks," I whispered.

"Don't mention it," he said, smiling.

I looked up to find Sergio staring at us.

28

Whats wrong?" I asked.
"The prophecy ..." he said. "Child of darkness, child of light ..."
I grinned.

"Don't you mean half-breed?" I asked.

My mom frowned. "Be polite, Katie," she said.

"It's okay, Libby," Sergio said to her. He continued to stare at our linked hands. "These two children are important to the future of our two peoples," he said, turning to my mom. "I wonder ..."

As he spoke, he pulled a book from an inner pocket of his long black coat. He looked down at it for a moment, and then placed it in my free hand. I looked at the cover. The writing on it looked strange—almost Egyptian, but not quite. And the pages were made of ...

"Linen?" I asked. "Is this book written on linen?"

My mother stepped forward.

"Let me see," she said, taking the book from me and holding it up to the light.

"This is ancient Etruscan," she said, turning to Sergio. "Where did you get this book?"

"The Velathri took it from Pompeii," he replied. "But we did not destroy it."

My dad shifted on the couch behind me. I turned to look at him and found his eyes were open.

"Dad?" I said.

"I'm here," he said. "How? I should be dead …" His voice trailed off as he pushed himself into a sitting position.

Sergio sat on the couch at my dad's feet. "Your daughter and her friend," Sergio said. "Their blood healed you."

"But that's not possible," my dad said, his voice stronger. He looked sharply at Johan, and then added, "Well, maybe it is."

"That must be why the Tuatha king gave him my staff," I said.

"What staff?" my mother interjected.

"My rowan staff, the one Ben and Colin gave me for my birthday."

My dad laughed.

"Yes, I would say it belongs to Johan, not you," he said, chuckling.

"Do you want to explain why?" I asked.

"There are rumors, well, there have always been rumors," Dad said.

"Rumors of what?"

"That the fairy king had children born of vampires. There are a few green-eyed vampires, but they appear around the world, not just in Ireland, so most of us just dismissed the rumors. I guess you and Alex aren't the only fairy-vampire children who survived."

Dad turned to Johan.

"Your father, for instance, was born in Germany," Dad said. "But the staff, well, I'd say that's proof."

"That must be what Breannan meant when he said my parents weren't the only ones keeping secrets," I said slowly.

My mom looked up from the book in her hands.

"Tony," she said. "Take a look at this."

"Yes," he breathed. "The first book, written before all of the others. Thought to have been destroyed by the Velathri centuries ago."

"We didn't dare destroy it," Sergio said. "It's too powerful. So we hid it. I've brought it to you because I want there to be peace between our peoples. And I believe these two children are an important part of that."

My dad looked from my face to Johan's. "Yes, that's quite possible."

"Many lives have been lost," Sergio said. "The Velathri and the Tuatha fought until the sun came up. The field will lie fallow for a hundred years because of the blood spilled there two nights ago."

He looked directly at me as he said it.

"Alex," I said. "Mom, I'm so sorry."

My mom blinked back tears.

"He died protecting you. I'll always be grateful to him for that," she said.

"I'm still confused," I said. "Who's been trying to kill me? The Tuatha protected me, and the Velathri have given us the book."

"That's why I'm here," Sergio said. "Fergus the Fierce has been playing a dangerous game. He's been systematically killing vampire-fairy children for centuries, and letting the Velathri and Tuatha think it was each other."

"Why would he do that?" I asked.

"To keep the treaty intact," Sergio said. "He is power-hungry and somewhat mad."

"So he's the one who sent the witch and the werewolves after me?" I asked.

"Yes, I was wrong when I thought the Tuatha were behind that. And now he's disappeared. We haven't been able to track him," Sergio said. "The Tuatha haven't been successful, either."

"How did you find out it was Fergus?" I asked.

"Your mother," Sergio said. "She tracked him from Rome to Ireland."

"He dropped in on the Tuatha, right before you got there," Mom said. "He left with the two werewolves who brought your staff to the king. I tracked them to the Giant's Causeway, but then they disappeared."

"Mom, you're a tracker?" I asked. My parents were full of surprises.

"Yes, and that's why I couldn't contact you to let you know where I was," Mom said. "I'm so sorry I missed your birthday, sweetheart."

"It's okay, Mom," I said, giving her a hug. "I know tracking Fergus was important. What did you find out?"

"I was in Rome with Claire, Adam, and Ariel. We had taken the werewolf that tried to kidnap you in the airport to the Garda Council there," Mom said. "But they were acting strangely. We thought they'd interrogate the werewolf, or at least imprison him, but they said he could go free. The more I thought about it, the more upset I got, so I went back to the council room to ask why. But on my way there, I saw Fergus the Fierce. I thought that was odd, so

I hid behind a column, and when he came out of the council room, the werewolf was with him, and they were talking and laughing. So I followed them. Another werewolf joined them outside of Rome, and they all headed to Volterra. The werewolves stayed outside of the city walls, but I followed when Fergus went in. He met with the Velathri triumvirate."

"Yes," Sergio said. "I was in the meeting. He told us the Tuatha were moving against us, and if we wanted to survive, we needed to strike first. I was against this, but the triumvirate believed him. They led a strike force to the Stone of Destiny."

"Yes, and it cost my brother his life," my mother said gravely. "What proof did he bring to convince them?"

"He had the book, *Rulers of Italy*. He said he'd gotten it from the Garda Council."

My dad gasped. "They *gave* it to him? What were they thinking?"

"I don't know what he told them to convince them to hand it over. It's now safe in Volterra," Sergio said. "*Rulers of Ireland* is in Montepulciano, and *A New World Order* is in your hands right now."

"I need to translate this book," Dad said.

"We intend for you to," Sergio replied. "Will you come with us to Volterra and translate the book there?"

"What about your bosses? The triumvirate?"

"The triumvirate no longer exists," Sergio said. "Two of them were killed in the battle with the Tuatha, and the third so severely injured he will never be the same. I am now the ruler of the Velathri. I need you, Tony. I need you to help me form a new government, one where Velathri and Stregoni work together, and we end this war with the Tuatha."

My dad broke the tense silence.

"I'll go to Volterra. I'll translate the book, and help you form a new vampire government. But on one condition."

"And what is that?"

"Katie must be allowed to stay here in Charleston, and complete her high school education at Saint Francis."

"She and Johan would be safer with us in Volterra," Sergio said.

"They'll be safe here," Dad said.

"I'll make sure of it," my mom said.

Sergio looked at each of us, his expression serious, then slowly nodded.

"Dad?" I asked. "Will you really be okay?"

My dad gave Sergio an appraising look.

"I trust Sergio," he said. "There are some others, however …"

"I'll go, too," Marc said, stepping forward. "I'll make certain he's safe."

"You will return to the city you hate?" Sergio asked, raising his eyebrows at Marc.

"For Tony, yes," Marc said. "His parents took me in when I was orphaned. I owe them a debt."

"Let's go, then," Sergio said. "Tony?"

Dad stood up and looked down at his bloody shirt.

"First, I need to clean up," he said.

"You know where the bathroom is," my mom said. "And some of your clothes are in the guestroom closet."

Dad headed upstairs to shower and change. Johan walked over to me. As I turned toward him, the front door flew open. Claire burst through, with Johan's parents behind her. Claire lifted her hand and sent a burst of white light at Sergio, knocking him to the ground.

"No, Claire, he's a friend," I yelled, jumping in front of a gasping Sergio.

"Of course you would think that," she spit at me, anger pulling her features tight. "You're one of them."

"Claire, he's got the third book! He can help us!"

"Alex is dead because of you!" she screamed, sending a blast of light toward me.

I braced, expecting to be knocked to the ground like Sergio. But my skin absorbed the light. I wasn't hurt. In fact, I felt stronger.

"I'm also one of you," I said calmly.

"I don't care!" Claire panted. "Fergus is right. Half-breeds shouldn't exist. Fairies and vampires have been enemies for millennia, and it's stupid to think that can change."

As I watched, her shape changed from the Claire I knew to a glowing woman.

"I could have spent the last seven years of my life with my husband," she spit at me. "But instead I spent it babysitting you. I am no longer your Garda. You're on your own."

And with that, she disappeared.

"What just happened?"

My dad came running down the stairs, hair still wet, to find our little group standing in shocked silence. Johan's parents had their arms around their son. My mom stood with her mouth open. Sergio grunted, and then pushed himself to his feet.

"I see not all fairies are happy about our alliance," he said dryly.

"I'm afraid Alex's death has upset her," Mom said.

"That's an understatement," I said. "She seems to think that if Alex is dead, all other fairy-vampire children should be, too."

"Then it's even more important that I translate the book," Dad said. "And the protective wards around the house and school need to be changed to keep Claire out."

My mom nodded. "I'll take care of it. The Meyers' house, too."

"What about Adam and Ariel?" I asked. "Do they think the same way Claire does?"

"We don't know yet," Mom said. "I'll set the wards to keep them out for now."

Dad turned and put his arms around me, hugging me close.

"Don't worry, Mia Bella," he said. "I'll be back next year to see you graduate."

I blinked back tears as I watched him walk out of the front door and into the dark with Marc and Sergio. As they went, I realized what I was looking at—the new triumvirate. A Velathri, a Stregoni Benefici, and a Velathri raised by Stregoni after his parents' death. Things were changing already, even before the third book was translated.

I was glad to be home, with my mom and Johan safely beside me. We were back where we'd begun, surrounded by family and friends. But things were different. I was different. I'd lost an uncle I'd never really had time to know. I'd lost my best friend. I'd lost any idea of what my future would be like. Or had I? I looked over at Johan. He smiled and reached out his hand. I grasped it, feeling both strength and gentleness in his grip.

I can do this, I thought. I'll learn how to be a vampire in a human world. I'll figure out how to stop a fairy-vampire war. I'll make it through my senior year without Claire. And maybe, just maybe, I'll beat Bryan Blalock in a race. And if my dad didn't show up for graduation, I'd go to Volterra and bring him back myself. But right now, I needed a shower and to sleep for a very long time.

EPILOGUE

I sat on the beach, watching the full moon rise over the ocean. A soft breeze brushed over my skin like warm velvet. I could smell salt water and marsh grass and the faint tang of boat fuel. I was finally wearing the black dress and my new black espadrilles—the ones I'd carried all over Europe and back again without even taking them out of my suitcase. Johan sat beside me, twisting a piece of marsh grass in his fingers.

We'd been out to dinner with his parents and my mom. We'd told them about our journey from Montepulciano to the Stone of Destiny and then back to Charleston. Edward and Juliana told us how the Tuatha had beaten back the Velathri, and how they'd tried to save Alex. My mom told us about tracking Fergus the Fierce from Rome to Volterra and on to Ireland.

Tomorrow was the first day of our senior year. Going to school without Claire was going to be difficult. I still missed her, and the thought that she hated me now was incredibly painful. I dreaded the questions I was sure to get from our classmates. Adam and Ariel hadn't returned to Charleston, and they had let my mom know they didn't intend to. Our story was that the family had returned to Ariel's home in France.

I can do this, I thought, leaning back and looking up at the full moon. Wait. Weren't full moons supposed to be dangerous?

ACKNOWLEDGMENTS

Many thanks to Mindy Kuhn and Amy Ashby of Warren Publishing for helping guide me through the process of turning a manuscript into a book, and to my talented niece Hana Russell for providing the perfect cover art.

I also owe a huge debt of gratitude to my incredible beta readers for being willing to wade through rewrite after rewrite: my mom Beth, sister Patience, daughter Mary, and best friend Beverly. Finally, I will be eternally grateful to the four people who believed in me even when I didn't believe in myself: Adam, Mary, Ben, and Hugh. You guys rock.

www.ingramcontent.com/pod-product-compliance
Lightning Source LLC
Chambersburg PA
CBHW031756260626
47154CB00027B/2450